I0744408
Penny

Penny

A BAY AREA DUET SERIES NOVELLA

PERSEPHONE AUTUMN

BETWEEN WORDS PUBLISHING LLC

Depths Awakened

One Night Forsaken

Every Thought Taken

Stone Bay Series

Broken Sky - Prequel Novella

Devotion Series

Distorted Devotion

Undying Devotion

Beloved Devotion

Darkest Devotion

Standalone Romance Novels

Sweet Tooth

Transcendental

Poetry Collections

Ink Veins

Broken Metronome

Slipping From Existence

PUBLISHED UNDER P. AUTUMN

Standalone Horror Novels

By Dawn

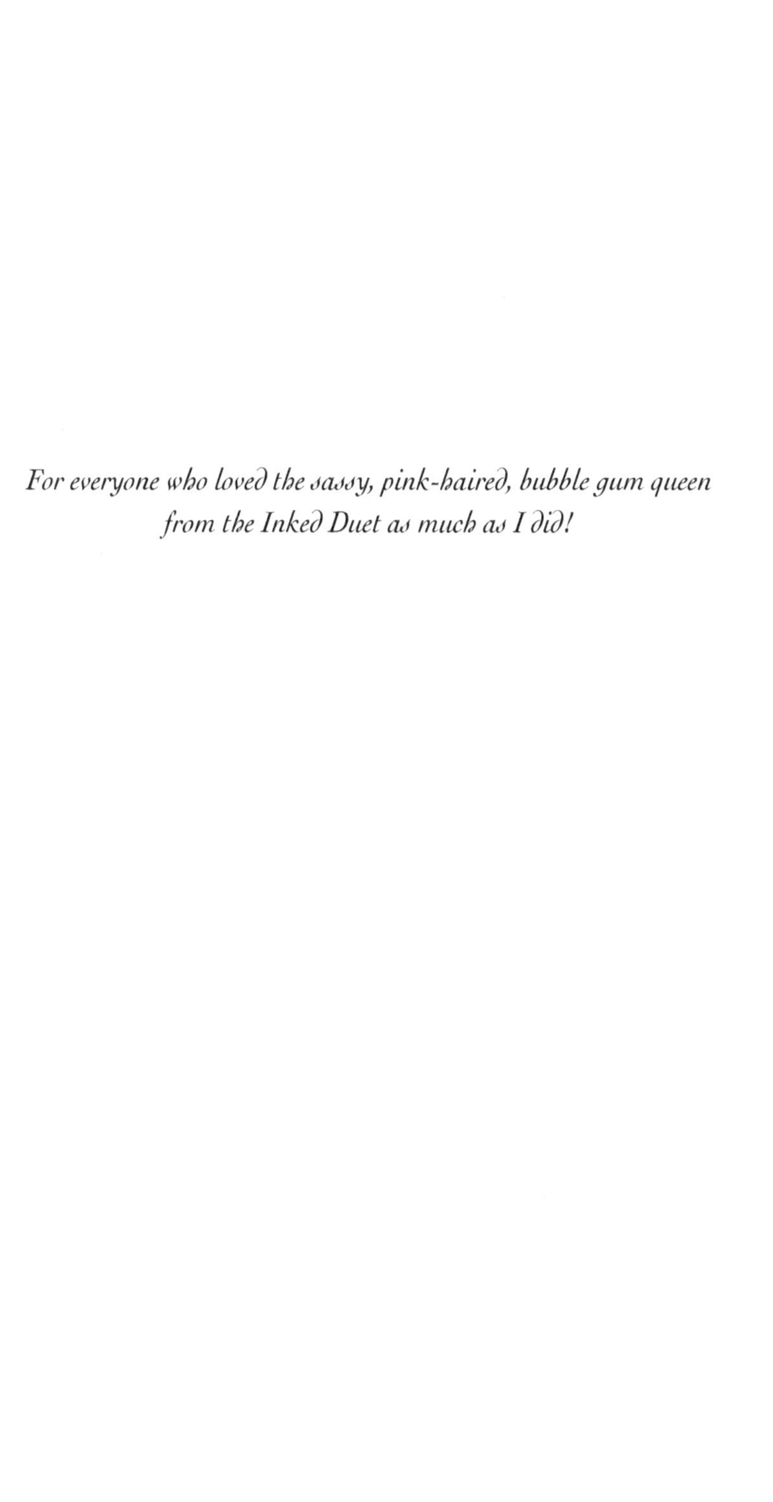

For everyone who loved the sassy, pink-haired, bubble gum queen from the Inked Duet as much as I did!

ONE

PENNY

THE DOOR SWINGS OPEN, THE BELL RINGING AS OSCAR steps in. Sweat beads his forehead and temples. In the thick of the July heat, sweat on anyone's brow wouldn't be odd. But I know my boss. He cranks the air conditioning as high and cold as possible March through November.

Why the hell is he sweating so much?

Popping my gum, I lean into Autumn and whisper, "Is it just me or does Oscar look nervous?"

Autumn regards Oscar as he steps farther into the shop, not making eye contact or greeting any of us. "Yeah, something is definitely off." She twists to face me. "Think he's okay?" She clamps her lips between her teeth. "It's odd he asked us all here on a Sunday."

Oscar's Tattoo Emporium has been my second home for the last twelve years. To say I know this place inside and out is an understatement. This place has seen thousands of clients. Won local awards for Best Tattoo Shop in the Bay Area for several years. Had a few artists come and go, but the core of our family has remained solid.

So when I study the man across the room, watch how his foot taps incessantly as he checks his phone every other breath, I know something isn't right.

As I open my mouth to ask Autumn what she thinks is happening, Oscar looks up and finally greets us.

"Hey, everyone." He lifts a hand in an awkward wave. "Sorry to steal part of your Sunday. This won't take long. Promise." He taps the screen of his phone, takes a deep breath, then stows it in his pocket. "I have news."

I stop breathing for one, two, three seconds.

With the nervous energy radiating off him, I have a sneaking suspicion the news is not good.

Oscar looks at each of us in turn as he works his jaw. "I'm selling the shop."

The room turns deathly quiet as we all register what he just said. When my brain connects his words with reality, I chew the gum in my mouth faster. Blow a bubble and stare at the man who hired me years ago. *He looks tired. Why haven't I noticed?*

I pop the bubble and blurt, "Why?"

All eyes dart to me, but I don't care. I need to know why my family is being sold. Well, *we* aren't being sold. Not really. Of all his recent visits, Oscar has given no hints he considered selling the shop. Either he has hidden it well or something happened with him or his family.

The corners of his eyes soften as Oscar regards me. "Penny, I'd love to run the shop until I stop breathing." His lips flatten for a beat. "But Chelle isn't doing well."

What happened to his wife? "She just had her annual checkup and the doctor found a growth on her ovary." He runs a hand through his hair. Pain mars his face as he scans the room. "I need to be there for her and Clarissa. As much as I love this place, the chain of shops, I need to sell. So I can be home."

Before he gets another word out, Autumn and I rush across the room to wrap him in our arms. Iliana, Rex, and Reznor surround us a beat later. We just hold this man. Give him strength when he needs it most. I may not like that he has to sell the shop, but I understand his reasons.

Oscar complains we are making him hot, then laughs as we break apart. "Thanks for the support. It means a lot." He rubs his hands together. "Part two." He winces. "The new owner will be here soon."

I groan and everyone else laughs.

Some people may say I am a bit much. Extra. Special. Those people would be correct. What can I say? I own who I am. I like what I like. And, nine times out of ten, I am a creature of habit.

No doubt Oscar did his homework before selling his business. Whoever the new owner is, they are probably as great as he is. Surely, he spoke with several buyers before choosing.

But I don't want someone new. I want Oscar. He is our family too.

"If I may…" Reznor lifts his hand like this is grade school and he needs permission to speak. Oscar tips his head at Reznor. "I also have news."

We all stare and wait. When he doesn't continue, I say, "Well, spit it out."

"Tatyana and I are pregnant again." The room erupts into cheers. "And I proposed." Autumn claps her hands over her mouth. "She said yes." Louder cheers fill the room. Congratulations shared with hugs. When the room settles again, he adds, "Which is why I was going to ask for fewer hours."

What. The. Shit is happening?

In less than ten minutes, it feels like our perfect little family is going in separate directions. And I am *not* okay with this. While everyone chats with Reznor, smiles plastered across their faces, I slowly melt inside. Metaphorically fall to the floor and curl into a ball.

I should be happy for Reznor. Should be excited for him, Tatyana, and Ashton. Should be smiling and asking if he knows if he will soon have a daughter or another son.

Instead, I stand paralyzed. Unable to muster up an ounce of joy for my friend.

Everyone is moving on.

Autumn and Jonas got married almost two months ago. They live in a beautiful house. Have a family. Reznor and Tatyana will be in the same position soon too.

Iliana hasn't mentioned any life-changing events. She lives a low-key life with her girlfriend, and their relationship is still young.

And Rex... well, Rex is just Rex. Once the roommate I wanted to throttle, he has matured since he took over Autumn's room in the apartment. Do I hate that we still share a bathroom? Absolutely. But at least I don't have to ask him to pick up his boxers and socks anymore. We also set up house rules for nights when either of us has company. Overall, he has been a great roommate.

"You okay?" Autumn asks as she sidles up to me by the reception counter.

"Yes. No." I stare back at my best friend. "I don't know." Exhaling, I shake my head. "Feels like everyone but me is moving forward."

"Oh, Pen." She wraps her arms around me and squeezes tightly. "We're all moving forward, just some of our paths have shifted. Yours will too."

"I'm not so sure." She unravels from the hug. "Not like anyone is knocking on my door, Auti."

We glance across the room at the guys and Iliana as they chat. Autumn clutches my hand. "You know I felt the same way before Jonas." She meets my gaze. "When it's meant to, change will happen for you too. Everything in its own time."

No matter how many times or how many ways I have heard that everything happens for a reason, I have yet to let it sink in. To root itself in my head and morph itself into truth. I *should* believe it. Autumn is proof. Maybe I don't believe it yet because I haven't been on the receiving end. Not yet.

I chew my gum and try to let in positive vibes. *Everything happens when it's meant to.* I blow a bubble so big, it blocks my line of sight. Just as I go to pop it, the bell over the front door jingles.

Shit. New boss.

I pop the bubble, tuck the gum in my cheek and drop

my gaze as I smooth my hands down my thighs. Had I known I was meeting a new boss today, I would've worn something besides denim cutoffs and a graphic tee. Not that we dress fancy here. Too late now.

A pair of black leather boots come into view as I finish chastising my own attire. Slowly, my eyes rake up a pair of denim-clad legs, a black button-up—sleeves rolled to the elbows exposing a full sleeve of tattoos on both arms—to meet the person who bought the shop from Oscar. My favorite shade of blue stares back at me and my jaw drops.

"Jameson?"

Jameson Kingsley. My brother's best friend. A guy I crushed on most of my adolescence and fantasized about occasionally in adulthood. This is my new boss.

Fuck.

TWO

JAMESON

WELL, WELL, WELL. IF THIS ISN'T THE BEST SURPRISE. I cock a brow and grin at the woman before me. The same woman who was checking me out seconds ago.

"Penelope," I say as I extend my hand. More than ever, I love the way my tongue flicks when I say her name. "Good to see you."

She slips her hand in mine. Warm, soft, and absolute perfection when cradled in mine. Her skin on mine feels different than it did years ago when I'd hung out with her brother and figured out every possible way to be near her.

"Penny," she corrects. "Good to see you, too, Jameson."

Several sets of eyes watch us, but I don't give a fuck. Let them think whatever. Everyone, including Penny, is lucky I haven't pulled her into an embarrassing hug.

Another time.

"Didn't know you worked here." She arches a brow in

disbelief. "Seriously. Had I known, no one else would've had a chance at this place."

"Wh-what?" she whisper-asks.

Reluctantly, I let go of her hand. "We'll talk more later."

Oscar walks me around the room and introduces me to the rest of the staff. The first thing I note is how few employees this shop has. Three artists and two receptionists. One of the artists also doubles as the store manager. With the listed shop hours, they have stretched themselves thin. I make a mental note to bring on at least one new artist, if not more, and two piercers.

When we reach Reznor, the artist who also manages the store in Oscar's absence, he relays his recent news and need for fewer hours.

"Do you still want the management role?"

His lips pucker to the side as he considers his answer. He shakes his head. "With a new baby on the way, it's probably best I forfeit the job. I won't be able to put in the hours."

I extend my hand, and we shake. "Thanks for being up front and straightforward, man. We'll work out the specifics soon. All I ask is that you stay on as manager until your replacement is ready. Shouldn't take long."

Reznor nods. "Of course."

Oscar and I move to the center of the room and spin to face the group. We explain the logistics of how the shop will transfer over the next two weeks. The legalities were handled before this meeting. All we have left to do is swap the name of the business—on signs, the website and business cards, and with vendors. Most are tedious, but will be done in a week or two.

Oscar plans to stay on during the transition to help the process flow as smoothly as possible. Talk with any long-time customers who express concerns about the change.

"My goal is to be transparent with each of you. If you have questions or concerns, let's put them on the table now. We may not have an instant solution, but we'll sort one out quickly." I scan the faces of the staff, trying my damnedest to not stay on Penny longer than suitable. When no one speaks up, I move on. "The shop needs more staff." I look over to Reznor. "With future changes coming, it's best to be prepared now. Another artist or two. Piercers. A new manager." Out of the corner of my eye, Penny pops her gum, then shakes her head. "Something you'd like to add, Penelope."

Her eyes shoot to mine and narrow. Penny doesn't hate her full name but uses it only when necessary. I use it to get under her skin… in all the right ways. I remember every time her skin pinked when I called her Penelope years ago. I also remember wondering if her skin grew flush *everywhere* when I used her full name.

I still want to know.

"Penny," she huffs out as she slaps her hands on her hips. "And I hope you don't plan to hire some schmuck off the street to be our new manager."

"Penny," the woman next to her whispers as her eyes widen.

"What, Auti?" She looks around at everyone, then pins me with her stare. "I get it. You bought the shop and things will change. Whatever. But don't bring in some rando off the street to dictate our jobs to us."

God, she is fire and sass. Honest and bold. Time has been good to her—physically and otherwise. And damn… she turns me the fuck on.

"So, Penelope." I smile as her lips form a tight line. "What do you propose?"

Her brows pinch at the middle. "Wh-what? Why are you asking me?"

Crossing my arms in front of me, I widen my stance. "You seem to have strong feelings about this. Only fair if you give suggestions."

Everyone goes silent. Autumn bites down on her lip to hide her smile. Iliana looks away to disguise the laughter she fights. And the guys… they seem highly fascinated with their shoes.

"I don't—"

"You," I say, cutting her off. Her eyes narrow in confusion. "Why don't I promote you?"

"Uh…"

I love that I render her speechless. That I solved a problem for both her and me, yet she has no comeback. No smart remarks and goofy faces. In addition, my favorite shade of pink colors her skin. The color not quite as brilliant as her hair but still as magnificent as ever.

Without thought, my eyes drop to her chest. Although covered, I picture the flesh between her breasts and collarbones just as pink.

Fuck, I need to leave.

I clap my hands. "It's settled." Turning, I extend a

hand and shake with Oscar. One by one, I shake everyone else's hand and tell them we will talk more during the week.

When I reach Penny, I offer my hand and she just looks at it. Stares without a word as if my touch may burn her. Who knows… maybe it will. And god would I love it if she is just as affected by me as I am her.

Seven slow and steady breaths later, she takes my hand, but we don't shake. I lean into her and drop my lips to her ear. Breathe deeply and sigh at the same artificial melon scent she has had for years. Watermelon Bubble Yum.

"Was a pleasure seeing you, Penny." I stroke her pulse with my finger and she shivers. "A real pleasure." Against my own desires, I lean back and straighten, drop her hand, and wink. "See you soon."

THREE

PENNY

Why did I have to open my big mouth? Why did I put myself in this predicament? Oh, right... because I didn't want some rando in the shop dictating our lives.

Elbows on the desk, I drop my head in my hands and stare down at the new stack of job applications and résumés Jameson left me to review. Every time I pick one up, a new wave of jitters rolls in my belly. The shop hasn't brought on anyone new since Iliana, and that was months after Autumn started. This place has been solid, a unit, for so long. The idea of adding new people to the mix has me nauseous.

What if they're an asshole? What if they do shitty work? What if they don't vibe with us?

All these scenarios, plus a hundred more, run through my head. I am not completely opposed to change, but too much is happening all at once. Oscar selling the shop to Jameson last month. The shop name change—King of Hearts Ink... full of yourself much, Kingsley? The constant calls and questions when our regulars saw the changes online.

I may be tough as nails and balls to the wall, but there is only so much a gal can handle at once.

As if he hears my inner turmoil through the office walls and throughout the shop, Reznor knocks on the open office door before stepping inside. He closes the door behind him, then takes a seat in the chair on the opposite side of the desk. The room remains silent for a beat, but I feel his gaze burning a hole in my head.

"Hey, Rez," I groan out, not lifting my head to look him in the eye.

"Penny, you know I love you. Right?" His words hesitant and quiet.

Inhaling deeply, I lift my head and lean back in the chair. Cross my arms over my chest. Narrow my eyes and study his expression a moment. "Yes," I say, drawing out the single-word response.

He squirms in the chair before leaning forward to rest his elbows on his knees. "If this is..." He takes a deep breath then meets my stare. "Not suggesting you can't handle this, but if it's too much—"

"If it's too much what, Rez?" He scratches the back of his neck. "Too much work for someone like me?" I point at the wall in the general direction of the reception desk in the lobby. "I may not have dealt with half this crap at the front desk, but that doesn't mean I can't handle it."

"God, Pen, I know." He leans back in the chair and looks away. Studies the photos on the office wall of us, our tattoo family, and the bright smiles we shared year after year. His eyes meet mine, a softness in his expression. "If anyone can conquer this place, it's you. But with all the changes in such a short period, even I'd be ready to rip my hair out."

"Please don't." I unlock my arms and rest my hands in my lap. "You have nice hair." My lips slowly tip up at the corners and we both laugh.

"Seriously, though." He finger-combs his hair. "I asked for fewer hours, but I don't mind helping out. Share the load until things settle more." He points to the stack of papers on the desk. "Want help weeding out interview candidates?"

I sit up, rake my eyes over the pile and sigh. "Is it horrible that I don't want to hire anyone?" My gaze lifts to meet his. "That I don't want to disrupt what we have here?"

Leaning forward, Reznor reaches across the desk and takes my hands in his. "It's not horrible. I get it. Really, I do. But at the end of the day, we need to bring in more people." He gives my hands a squeeze then releases them. "Autumn and I both work way less now. Our lives are different. Leaving Rex to pick up the rest of the slack isn't fair." He shakes his head, then says, "He won't be mad about the extra income, but he'll burn out before long. Then, we'll be in a jam."

I groan and Reznor chuckles. Pointing a finger at him, I say, "You know I hate it when you make a valid point." I really don't hate it. More like I hate that I am too scared to say the exact same. To own the changes that need to happen. "Thank you for offering to help." I pick up the applications and tap the bottom of the stack against the desk. "Maybe I just needed to vent." He arches a brow. "But I got this. Go." I jerk my chin toward the shop. "Ink some skin."

He lingers in the chair a beat before rising to his feet. Without a word, he shuffles toward the door and through the threshold. But before he is out of sight, he turns and says, "We're a family, Pen. It's okay to lean on us."

I nod with a smile and he walks off.

Reznor checking in with me was exactly what I needed. Someone who cares showing support. Someone who has sat in this very chair and done everything—minus the interviews—I am doing now, plus work in the shop. If he can manage all the roles, so can I.

I thumb through the applications and attached résumés with renewed purpose. Take a deep breath and look at the bigger picture. Yes, I love our little family as it is. But Reznor made a good point. Not bringing in new people only punishes us. And that, I am not okay with.

I stand and extend my hand across the desk. "It was wonderful meeting you, Sage. We'll be in touch." Sage shakes my hand as she rises from the chair.

"Thank you. If you have any other questions, please call. Anytime."

She shoulders her purse, and I walk her out of the office to the front door. When I spin around, three sets of eyes pin me in place. I smile and give an enthusiastic thumbs-up before heading back to the office. Back to where Jameson waits to discuss the interview he sat in on.

I breeze past everyone, dart inside the office and shut the door. Much as I don't want to be in a confined space with Hotty McHotterson, I also don't want to answer everyone's questions about the interview. Not yet. Need to digest it all myself first.

"I like her," Jameson states as I take my seat.

God, he is close. Too close. Why is he sitting right there?

I peer to my left but don't fully face him. If I spin the chair, my knees will knock his legs. And physical contact with Jameson… that is a no-no.

"Do you now?"

A smile kicks up one corner of his mouth and he winks. "Not how I like you, BYP."

BYP. How many years have passed since I heard that nickname? Several. Enzo stopped using it when he graduated high school and moved out of the house. Since then, I have been Pen or Penny.

At the time, I missed the cute term of endearment. Missed my playful brother. But he'd done his best to act mature. To show my parents he could adult on his own. For years, I wanted to tell Enzo nicknames didn't make you immature. If anything, they show you care.

So what does it mean that Jameson just used my childhood nickname? The Bubble Yum Princess. BYP. Is he being playful?

God, he used to give me so much shit. Teased me about my clothes and the way I wore my hair.

In turn, I gave him a hard time. Called him out.

"Funny that you tease me. Especially considering you hang out with people who dress and act just like me."

He played it off. Every single time.

Except that one time. The time I told him his girlfriend at the time looked like an older version of me. Yeah, that shut him down real quick. I didn't see him for months. Enzo hung at Jameson's house after school or they met up elsewhere.

In my teenage brain, I didn't pay attention to what it all meant. The jokes and banter. The fact that he stopped coming to the house after that comment. Or the fact that his girlfriend at the time was an older version of me with purple hair instead of pink.

But now…

Oh. My. Fucking. God.

I swallow past the sudden dryness in my throat. "BYP, huh?"

He nods. "The one and only."

"Hmm. Can't argue with that." Without thinking, I swivel the chair. My knee brushes the outside of his thigh and, for five minute-long seconds, I don't breathe. Jameson appears to forget how as well. I blink and clear my throat. "Don't you…" Voice as hoarse as if I'd been center stage at a concert, I swallow once, then twice, and start again. "Don't you think I've outgrown such childish names?"

My knee is still pressed to the side of his thigh. Such light pressure, yet it feels monumental. The fact that neither of us backs away or shifts from the contact has me sweating in awkward places. His tongue darting out and licking his lips also doesn't help the cause.

"What do you propose I call you instead?" Challenge laces his voice as he brings his hand to his jaw and toys with his beard.

Don't stare. Don't freaking stare. But my eyes refuse to look away as he strokes his beard. *Damnit, Penny! Get a hold of yourself!*

"You're a big boy, Kingsley," I say, bolder than I feel. Against every hormonal cry in my body to keep touching him, I swivel the chair away and face forward. I despise the immediate gooseflesh on my arms and legs. Loathe the whimper that wants to crawl up my throat and exit my lips. *Get. It. Together.* "Sure you'll figure something out."

He goes quiet for a beat. Too quiet. I pick up Sage's résumé and pretend to read over it. Pretend like I have lost interest in his little game.

Until his breath is on my ear. "I may have something up my sleeve."

The urge to face him heats my skin. But I don't dare. I may not see him in my periphery, but I *feel* him. If I move the slightest bit, his lips will be a breath from mine. I close my eyes, take a deep breath and swallow.

"Bet you do," I mutter, then clear my throat. "Should we discuss Sage?"

He chuckles under his breath as his chair creaks under the shift of his weight. I should be relieved he gave me room to breathe. But my traitorous body leans an inch to the left, begging for a smidge of his personal bubble.

Stupid. Freaking. Hormones.

"Yes, Penelope. Let's discuss Sage." Then his leg bumps my chair.

Why? Of all the people to buy Oscar's shop, why did it have to be Jameson Kingsley? Ooh, I know… because the universe loves to torture me.

Well, consider me tortured.

FOUR

PENNY

"UGH!" I HUFF OUT. "I'M AT MY WITS' END, AUTI. There's just too much damn testosterone in my life." Next to me, Autumn laughs with a shake of her head. *She laughs*. Some best friend.

"Sorry," she says between fits of laughter. She holds up her hand. "Really, I am."

I narrow my eyes at her. "Mm-hmm. Maybe I'd believe you if you *weren't laughing at me*."

Snagging the licorice and bucket of popcorn in her hands, I face the television and shove the snacks in my mouth. I do my damnedest to ignore her as she holds her stomach and works to halt her laughter. Focus my attention on Rory and Jess on the screen. Imagine I live in Stars Hollow and Lorelai is my neighbor and best friend. She'd be a fun person to have around.

"I'm sorry, Pen," Autumn says more seriously. "If our roles were reversed, you know you'd laugh at me too." I roll my eyes because she isn't wrong. She sets a hand on my thigh and lays her head on my shoulder. "I miss this. Sitting on the couch and watching *Gilmore Girls* on repeat while eating junk."

I lay my head on hers. "Me too. But you have it pretty damn good with Jonas and the kids."

She nods. "I do. But I miss nights like this. Girl time." She plucks a Twizzler from the bag. "We need to do this more. Just the two of us."

"Agreed."

Through the rest of the episode, we stay like this. Cuddled into each other, stuffing our faces with candy and popcorn. The next episode starts and Autumn hits pause. She excuses herself to use the bathroom and asks if I want anything while she is up. I wave her off.

I tug my phone from my back pocket and go through notifications while I wait. Swiping down on the home screen, I review and swipe away each one. *Email. Email. Target sale. Netflix show alert.* Just as I am about to swipe away the Instagram notification, I stop.

Jameson Kingsley has requested to follow you.

I blink down at the screen. Narrow my eyes as if my contacts are deceiving me. I blink again. Nope, still there. Beneath it, the next notification is for Facebook.

Jameson Kingsley sent you a friend request.

Autumn plops back down beside me, but I don't move. Don't look up at her.

"Everything alright?"

After a beat, I break contact with the screen, look her

in the eyes and slowly shake my head. I hold up my phone and show her the notifications.

"Could be nothing," she says. "You know him. He's our boss and part of the family now. It could be completely innocent."

I wish that were true, but it feels much more than innocent. Years may have passed since Jameson and I have been around one another, but this doesn't feel like an old friend or my new boss just connecting on social media. Every interaction with him since the moment he walked in the shop has had double meaning. To everyone else, his actions may seem harmless. An old friend of the family happy to see me again.

But they don't know Jameson Kingsley like I do. They don't see the way he looks at me with mischief in his eyes. They don't feel the hum under my skin every time he stands in the same room as me.

"What if it's not?"

The television screensaver kicks on as I ramble to Autumn about Jameson. About my childhood crush who teased me with a smirk on his face. The guy who spent almost every day in my house until I opened my mouth about his girlfriend's uncanny resemblance to yours truly. The man that has flirted with me at every possible opportunity since he bought the shop. How close he has been during each interview—staying professional while the candidate is present but dropping the facade as soon as we are alone. Most of all, I tell Autumn how his proximity has me in knots. How it jumbles my brain. How it renders me speechless.

When I finish, her lips tip up in a gentle smile. One that I would normally find endearing if it were directed elsewhere. But this sweet smile feels different somehow. Heavy. Loaded. Significant.

"What?" I ask when she doesn't say anything.

This only makes her smile grow more. I open my mouth to tell her I am leaving if she doesn't fess up, but her hand on my arm stops me with a gentle squeeze.

"It's okay to like him, Pen."

"I don't." The lie tastes bitter on my tongue.

"You do, and it's okay." I shake my head. "It is. He may be our boss, but we work in a different world than most people. There's no human resources person shaking a finger at you for inappropriate behavior. There's no one casting judgment or whining about disadvantage because you and the boss are dating."

"We aren't dating," I blurt out.

She shakes her head. "True, but it'd be okay if you were." She tucks her feet under her butt and twists to look me in the eye. "Pen, I missed out on so much because I was afraid to put myself out there. Hell, with as many times as I tried to push him away, I almost missed out on Jonas." Her eyes dart between mine. "If you like him, be open to the possibility of more."

"What if it goes to shit? I'd still have to work with him."

Autumn grips my shoulders with fierce strength. "What if it's perfect? What if it's the best decision you've ever made?" When I don't respond, the corners of her mouth slowly kick up. "Don't question it. Go with it."

"I don't want to be one of those women…" I pause and Autumn tilts her head in question. "The type who lose who they are because they're infatuated with some guy."

At this, she laughs. I try to shrug out of her touch, but she doesn't allow it. She holds on tighter.

"Penelope Jane, the day you lose yourself to a man is the day the world stops spinning." She shakes her head on another laugh. "No man will steal your light. No man will steal your throne." She grips my chin. "If anything, the right man will kneel before you. Worship the ground you walk on. Be proud to call you his."

Her words grow like vines in my mind. Take over every thought and weave through every scenario.

For the first time in my adult life, I consider the possibility of a serious relationship. Something beyond flirting and fun. Is that even possible with Jameson? His girlfriends never lasted more than a month or two when we were younger. Is he still like that? Get what he wants then hightail it out the back door.

Enzo would know, but I have zero intention of asking my brother about his best friend's relationship history. That would open the door to questions I do *not* want to answer.

"I see you spinning every worst-case scenario. You'll go up in smoke if you're not careful." Autumn laughs.

I twist and face her. "What would you do if you were in my position?"

She clamps her lips between her teeth and rocks her jaw side to side. "If what you feel is anything remotely close to how I felt when I first met Jonas, I'd take the leap. Jump in headfirst."

Take the leap. Jump in headfirst.

Can I do that? Can I give in to what I feel for Jameson?

I want to. More than I care to admit.

FIVE

JAMESON

"You what?"

This is not the reaction I expected from Enzo. Not by a long shot.

"I bought the tattoo shop Penny works at." My hands fly up to either side of my head. "In all fairness, I didn't know she worked there until Oscar and I signed the paperwork and he invited me to meet the staff." Enzo narrows his eyes, and I can't help but see the resemblance to Penny when he does it. "Swear."

Enzo and I have been friends more years than not. We met during the awkward middle school stage when girls became something other than annoying and our voices did that embarrassing squeak.

The two of us have done some crazy shit in the past. From dressing up the school mascot statue in a naughty-nurse costume to spiking the punch at the school dance with his dad's favorite single malt. I spent several years in his bedroom, playing video games and talking about shit we never told anyone else.

Lorenzo Singleton is my best friend. Always will be.

So why I never mentioned to him the idea of purchasing a tattoo shop is beyond me. Not like he wouldn't have backed up the idea. He would have been excited. Would have told me it was a solid investment.

If I would have told him.

"Fine," he huffs out. "I believe you." The doorbell rings, and he holds up a finger as he rises from the couch. "We're not done talking about this."

"Yes, dear," I joke as he walks off. His middle finger shoots up over his shoulder.

While he answers the door, I question why I didn't say anything to him. Why I didn't share what I wanted to do with the money Dad left me when he passed. Why I didn't get my best friend's opinion on such a life-altering decision.

"Life's too short. Do what makes you happy. Take risks. Fall in love. See the world."

The last words my father spoke to me play in my head for the millionth time. When he'd said them, I'd told him to quit talking like the pneumonia would win. That he'd be better the next day and leave the hospital soon. The next day, Mom and I tiptoed into his hospital room, not wanting to wake him. Less than an hour later, the machines went haywire. The squeal of the alarm bounced off the walls and embedded itself in my memory. Nurses rushed the room, and I stopped breathing as my father gasped for his own breath. Everything in that moment blurred from existence, everything but the sound telling us his heart stopped beating.

They say my father died peacefully. That his brain and body shut down as he drowned in his own fluids. But no matter how much they tried to convince me and Mom, I never believed it.

After he passed, I tried to live by his last words. Tried to live up to the man I had admired my entire life. I did what made me happy, what brought me joy. Tattoos happen to be one of those things.

And while I was at the tattoo convention last year, I overheard artists talking about buying their own shops. As I sat in the chair and got new ink, I asked how one would go about buying a shop. How I would find someone who wants to sell. Like anything, there was a website.

For months, I checked the site. Waited for a local shop to pop up. A little over three months ago, Oscar posted he was looking to sell. He had several shops but was willing to sell them individually. Without hesitation, I jumped. Took the risk with zero regrets.

Enzo walks back into the room with a pizza box and bag. He sets them on the coffee table and retakes his seat next to me on the couch. "Dinner is served."

He flicks on the television, opens Hulu and clicks on *American Horror Story*. We dive in, stuffing ourselves with pizza, garlic knots and beer. Halfway through the episode, my shoulders loosen up. When we both pick up our last piece and he still hasn't broached the subject of the shop again, I breathe easier.

The episode ends and I pat my belly. "Thanks for dinner, bro."

"No problem."

He gathers the trash and takes it to the kitchen. When he returns, it's with two more beers and a raised brow.

Damnit. Thought I lucked out.

"What?" I ask, feigning innocence.

"Two things." He holds up two fingers for emphasis. "One… why didn't you tell me you wanted to buy a tattoo shop? Feels like you left me stranded on a highway." His hand claps my shoulder. "You're my brother. We talk about everything."

We do talk about everything. Well, almost everything. But I have a sneaking suspicion it will all be on the table before I walk out the door tonight.

"After Dad died last year, I was in such a funk." He nods but doesn't interrupt. I go on to explain how I overheard artists at the tattoo convention. How I asked where to find shops for sale. "Early May, a local shop popped up. I looked into the owner, spoke with him on the phone and we set up a meet. It all went pretty quick." I shrug. "As to why I never told you… I don't know. Maybe because it felt like I was doing what Dad wanted me to. Taking a risk. If I would've said something, maybe you would've talked me out of it."

Enzo sips his beer and tips his head side to side. He tips the neck of the bottle in my direction. "Probably right." After another sip, he says, "But now that we've cleared that up, don't do that shit again."

I nod on a laugh. "Yes, dear."

When the room quiets again, his expression turns serious. His eyes lock on mine. "Two… what is your intention with my sister?"

I startle at the question. Every muscle inside me freezes. I open my mouth to answer but snap it shut, unsure of what to say. Do I *know* the answer?

Without question, I like Penny. More than either she or Enzo probably want to hear. Not sure when it happened, but early on, I stopped looking at her like my best friend's little sister and started seeing her as someone I wanted more with. To hold her, kiss her, call her mine.

With Penny, though, it isn't that simple. If I fucked up, Enzo would have my balls. And I really didn't want to fuck things up with her.

So, I held off. Dated other girls. Girls that reminded me of her in one way or another. The day she called me on it, I freaked out. Avoided her at all costs.

Now, though… life is different. *I* am different.

"Would you be pissed if I asked her out?"

His jaw tightens and I swear I hear his molars grind. "If you hurt her…"

"Never."

"What about her job? Last thing she needs is judgment or fear of losing her job if things go south."

I sigh and shake my head. "Do you really think so little of me?" He opens his mouth, but I speak before he does. "First off, I promoted her. The shop needs more staff, but she didn't want an outsider managing the place. So I gave her the position. Second, I would never do anything to jeopardize her job. Fuck you for thinking I would. And last, I have no clue if she'll even say yes to going out."

"She'll say yes."

I sit slack-jawed for a beat. "How can you be so sure?"

He sips his beer. A larger-than-life smile splits his face in half. "Because I know my sister."

Obviously, I am out of the loop on something. Either that or willfully blind to what is in front of me.

Green eyes, just a little different than my favorite pair, bore a hole in my head. "Let me reiterate. Make myself crystal fucking clear." He tips the bottle toward me again. "If you hurt her, in any capacity, I will fuck you up. We may be brothers, but she is my only sister. And no one fucks with her."

Message received.

"On my life, I won't hurt her."

SIX

PENNY

I SAG INTO THE CHAIR, TIP MY HEAD BACK AND SIGH AT the ceiling. "Hallelujah!" On the other side of the desk, Jameson laughs. My head pops back up, and I give him what feels like a menacing look. Knowing my luck, I look constipated. "Are you laughing at me, Kingsley?"

His hands fly up in surrender. "Don't shoot." He curbs his laughter. "I mean no harm." For shiggles, I throw a pen at him. "Hey! What'd that pen ever do to you?"

As he bends in the chair to find the pen, I take a moment to breathe. To let the calm settle in my bones for the first time in weeks. To feel relief flow through my bloodstream as all the major changes smooth out.

Damn it feels good to have balance again. To have things falling into place.

After more than a dozen artist, piercer and front desk interviews, Jameson and I decided who we want to offer jobs. Took hours of rehashing the interviews, but I believe they will make great additions. Deciding was more difficult than I thought it would be. Introducing new faces to a tight-knit group is a big deal. Making sure each of them fit in with us was vital.

"When do you want to call them?" I ask as Jameson sits up.

"Monday. Let's enjoy the weekend and worry about paperwork when it's over."

I peek up at the clock over his head and am shocked by the time. Almost six. Where the hell did the day go? Jameson walked in with lunch around noon and we've been holed up in here since, debating over our choices. What this room needs is a damn window. Something to show the sun as it moves east to west. Something to keep me from losing track.

Staring at the north wall, the one on the back of the building, I mumble, "Right there."

"Right where?" Jameson's eyes sear my profile. "And dare I ask what?"

I spin to face him and cock a brow. "There." I point at the wall and he looks at the collection of framed photos. "This room needs a window. Big. Small. I don't care. Just some damn sunshine."

He pinches his chin between his thumb and forefinger as he stares at the space in question. Then he strokes his beard, and I avert my gaze briefly.

Why? Why the hell does that one particular action make me gooey inside? It never has with anyone else. Ever.

"Might make things tight in here when I bring in another desk, but I'll make it work."

My eyes drop to the desk and roam the surface. A few dents and scratches mar the surface, but otherwise the desk is in great shape. Maybe he prefers more modern furniture. But newer pieces aren't made with the same craftsmanship. Being that Jameson spent so much time with my family years ago and how much my dad talked about quality woodwork, you'd think he wouldn't buy assemble-yourself furniture.

"I like this desk," I tell him. "It has character and good bones."

"Couldn't agree more."

"Then why are you replacing it?"

He stares at me for three, two, one. "I'm not," he answers hesitantly. "The other desk is for me."

What the what?

I lift a hand to my ear, insert a finger, and wiggle. "Sorry. Think I misheard you. Sounded like you said you'll have a desk in here too."

A smirk tugs at the corner of his mouth, and I want to smack it off. Cocky ass.

"Oh, you heard me correctly." He waves a hand around the fifteen-by-fifteen space. "It'll be tight, but we'll make it work."

"Why do you need a desk in here?"

He cocks his head and just stares at me for a moment. Part of me wants to bolt from the chair, stomp around the desk and shake his shoulders. Demand he answer me now. But I suppress the urge. Instead, I hold his gaze and play along with his waiting game.

"Afraid you won't get much work done with me here?"

Yes. "No."

That cocky smile makes another appearance. I love and hate it.

He shakes his head and laughs. "Shouldn't I have a place to work in my own business?"

"Oscar was almost never here."

"I'm not Oscar."

This much I know.

"How often will you be here?"

"Why does this feel like an inquisition?"

"Do you like answering questions with questions?"

He laughs harder this time. "I won't be here all the time, but I do want my hands in the business I just sank a lot of money in." Honestly, it makes sense. Owners should be hands-on if possible. "And since you're the only manager, I should be here when you need time off." He leans forward and rests his forearms on the desk. "You work hard, Pen. But you don't need to dig yourself an early grave. So, please, let me help."

Moments like this, when Jameson softens those bright-blue eyes, I lose all sense of direction. My motor skills... out the door. Every now and again, this man turns me to rubber. Has me bending to his will.

"You're right."

He cups his ear and leans closer. "Sorry, what was that?"

I throw the pen again and hit my desired target—his forehead. "Ass. You heard me."

"Ow," he says, then laughs as he rubs his forehead.

Pushing out my lower lip, I tease, "Aw. Poor baby has a boo-boo."

In a blink, the room turns utterly silent. Jameson looks across the desk, his eyes on my lips as he licks his own. And damn, if it isn't hotter than the summer sun outside. I swallow and his eyes drop to follow the action. I don't know what to think, to feel, to do. My pulse pounds, pounds, pounds in my chest. Whooshes behind my ears. And I swear to god, I might be panting.

Please don't let me be panting.

"Go on a date with me."

My brows pinch at the middle as his words slowly register. "What?"

"Go on a—"

"No, I heard you." I shake my head. Try to make sense of what he said. Because Jameson Kingsley asking me on a date… how many times did I envision this moment? I am too embarrassed to admit the answer. But I never thought it'd actually happen. Sure, Autumn and I talked about the possibility. If I'm honest, I thought I'd have to pull a Sadie Hawkins. "Why?" I finally ask.

"Really?" I nod and he bites his lower lip. "Am I not obvious enough?"

Yes, he had been obvious with his interest. But I also saw him through a different lens. One a bit rosier.

I shrug. "Maybe. Maybe not. My perception of things might be a bit misconstrued."

He licks his lips then smiles when my eyes follow the action for a split second. "Why is that?"

"Am I not obvious enough?" I throw his question back at him.

"Go on a date with me, Pen."

I don't move an inch as we stare at each other. My heart bangs against my rib cage, begging me to spit out the three-letter word. Begging me for relief. It would be so easy. Saying yes. Getting swept up in Jameson. Because I have wanted nothing more for several years.

Take the leap. Jump in headfirst.

"Yes."

"Yes?" I nod and the most brilliant smile lights his face. "Can I text you later? We'll sort out details." Again, I nod. He rises from his seat and reaches for my hand, bringing it to his lips. "Talk to you later, BYP." He winks, drops my hand, and exits the office.

"Yeah," I whisper to myself. "Talk to you later."

SEVEN

JAMESON

Never thought she'd say yes.

Penelope Singleton. The girl—woman—that tattooed herself on my heart long before I understood what it meant. The woman that I looked for in every person I dated. The woman that always lingered in the back of my mind.

No woman holds a candle to Penelope Singleton. And she said yes. To me.

God… I was prepared to beg. Prepared to emasculate myself. Lucky for me, it never came to that. She would have loved seeing me grovel. Savored it. Referred back to it for years.

I button up my shirt and roll the cuffs to my elbows. Leave it untucked from my jeans. Swipe product through my hair and beard, then comb both. Spritz cologne on my shirt—the one Dad always used and swore it was the only reason Mom never left. Then I take one last look in the mirror.

"Lucky bastard," I tell my reflection.

Pocketing my phone and wallet, I swipe my keys from the dresser and walk out the front door. Last night, a few hours after Penny said yes, my fingers hovered the phone keyboard until the screen dimmed. Twice. I typed and deleted and repeated more times than I care to admit. The reality of setting up a date with Penny made basic bodily functions forget their purpose.

Penny makes me dizzy in all the right ways. Throws my world off its axis. Makes me feel alive. And after not existing in her orbit for so long, I pray her gravity never releases me.

I weave through the city streets and drive toward Dunedin. Much as I wanted to knock on Penny's door, thread my fingers with hers and drive us to the restaurant, I also didn't want to make our first date awkward. Because it very well could be. Although a gap of time exists between now and high school, we know each other well. Really well. My one hope is that the time apart works in our favor.

Penny may have been like a little sister in the beginning, but the ideal didn't stick for long. Enzo would have throttled me had he known.

Tonight, my sole desire is to sit across from this bewitching woman and get to know who she is now. Hear about the years of her life I missed—not that Enzo never mentioned her. And if I'm lucky, by the end of the night, she won't see me as her brother's best friend. Hopefully, she will see me as someone at her side.

I park in the lot a block from the restaurant. As I reach

the sidewalk, I spot a pink old-school Cadillac convertible. Without a doubt, I know Penny owns the car. Pink and vintage are her calling card.

Twenty feet from the restaurant, I spot her and come to a halt. Head down, eyes on her phone. Victory rolls pinned in place while the length of her hair trails her spine. A red-and-white sleeveless top that looks more like a corset, ties at the nape of her neck. Tattoos on full display. Dark denim hugging her legs from hip to heel.

Goddamn.

As if she senses my presence, her eyes scan the sidewalk and land on my profile. A soft smile tips up the corners of her red lips. Eyes on me, she stows her phone and holds up a hand.

Deep breaths, King. Deep breaths.

One foot in front of the other, I close the space between us. My eyes never leaving hers. Heart pounding harder with each step forward. Blood humming in my veins as I reach her side.

"Hey," I say. "Sorry I kept you waiting."

With a shake of her head, her smile widens. "You didn't. I got here a few minutes ago."

"You look incredible." I scan her head to toe now that I have a better view. *Damn.*

She reaches up and toys with my collar. "As do you."

I gesture to the door. "Shall we?"

We step inside the restaurant and I fight the need to rest my hand on her lower back. *Too soon.* The hostess seats us in the outdoor area, hands us menus and relays the specials before leaving the table. Music plays from hidden speakers in the courtyard. Soft light glows from bulbs strung between the trees and fence enclosure. The summer breeze doing nothing to alleviate the nervous energy beneath my diaphragm.

The server sets a larger bottle of water on the table and takes our order. Penny orders a dish with squid ink pasta and seafood while I get the Korean beef tacos. Soon as the server walks off and the menus are no longer a distraction, my pulse pounds in my chest.

What the hell do we talk about?

Penny sips her water, leans back in her chair and makes me her point of focus. Setting the glass on the table, she toys with the rim as her eyes hold mine.

Damn, she makes me nervous. More than anyone.

"I realize it's summer…" Her lips shift to fight a smile. "When is it not summer here?" She laughs. "But you're sweating an awful lot. You okay?"

Swiping my glass from the table, I down half the water then mimic her posture. *Calm the hell down, King.* "On a date with Penny Singleton, what man wouldn't sweat his ass off?"

Her fingers freeze on the rim of the glass as she regards me and processes what I said. She sits up, moves the glass from between us and leans in my direction. If I follow her lead, her lips would be a breath from mine. Red and irresistible. Lips I've wanted pressed to my own. Lips I've fantasized about in more ways than one.

"Do you know why I said yes?" Her question makes me mentally stumble. I shake my head and her red lips kick up at the corners. "Either you're the master of disguise or completely oblivious."

God, I want to lean into her. Make her breath catch and pulse erratic. Make her body feel half the jitters coursing through my veins.

"Consider me in the dark."

Her tongue darts out and sweeps her lips. I fist my jeans under the table and suppress the moan in my throat. What is it about this woman that makes the world wobble beneath my feet?

"Jameson Kingsley, I'm shocked," she says, resting her palm over her heart. "I mean… I did my best to mask how I felt." She looks off in the distance, lips trapped between her teeth, jaw rocking side to side. Then soft-green irises meet mine and resume their focus. Her expression serious as her cheeks and neck flush. "But you had to have known."

I straighten in my seat, but leave little distance between us. "Known what, Penny?"

The pink tinting her cheeks darkens as she swallows. "That I had a crush on you." Her whispered words barely audible, but I hear them loud and clear.

Leaning closer, I buck up the courage and ask, "Had?"

She rolls her eyes. "Had. Have." Light laughter spills from her lips. "Tomato, tomahto."

I inch closer to her. Wipe my sweaty palms on my jeans. Lick my lips as I stare at hers. "What if I said the same?" Her brows pinch in confusion. "That I had it bad for you."

"Not sure I'd believe you," she says breathily.

Just as I open my mouth to spill every truth, the server steps up to the table with our dinner. The table falls silent as we eat our meals. Both of us mulling over this newfound information. When the server clears our plates and offers dessert, my lips want to say no while my heart refuses to deny what she wants. We split a slice of key lime pie, and it is the best damn pie I've ever eaten.

After I pay the check, we exit the restaurant and walk toward the lot. Unexpectedly, Penny laces her fingers with mine. I stop breathing. A rush of adrenaline spikes my bloodstream and has me floating with the stars.

"This okay?" she asks, squeezing my hand.

We reach her car and I drop my gaze to hers. "More than okay," I choke out. For a moment, we simply stand there, gazes locked and hands clasped. Before I lose the courage, before I let my nerves get the best of me, I ask, "Can I kiss you?"

She sucks in a breath. Her eyes dart between mine. Then, ever so slowly, she nods.

Not wanting to rush this, not with Penny, I lower my mouth to hers and sigh when we connect. Soft and warm and better than I imagined. My hand cups her jaw as I kiss her, slow and sweet. As I savor the moment. I don't push for more and break the kiss sooner than preferable.

I rest my forehead on hers. "I really like you, Penelope Singleton."

Her hand rests over my heart. "I really like you too, Jameson Kingsley."

I press a chaste kiss to her lips and reluctantly step

back. "Hey, Penny?" I lift her hand to my lips and kiss her knuckles. "Wanna go steady?"

A smile plumps her cheeks as she rolls her eyes. "Under one condition." I cock a brow. "I get to be the Queen of hearts."

I step back into her and crash my lips to hers. "You always have been." Truer words have never been spoken.

EIGHT

PENNY

I SPENT MOST OF SUNDAY CHATTING AUTUMN'S EAR OFF about my date with Jameson. The way he looked at me on the sidewalk. How he was dressed. Our confessions before the waiter interrupted. The kiss and him asking to be my boyfriend.

God, it was dreamy and surreal.

The first half hour, it irritated me not seeing her facial expressions. Autumn is always so expressive in person. She probably grinned or clamped her lips shut more often than not. But after a while, I stopped caring, and she said she was happy for me.

The rest of Sunday, I cleaned while *Gilmore Girls* played in the background. Threw out the leftovers that were slowly making new friends in the fridge. Wiped down every surface in the apartment. Vacuumed the living room, hallway and my bedroom. Washed the dirty clothes in the hamper plus my bedding. Reorganized my makeup in the bathroom.

I did everything possible to not check my phone. To look for missed texts or calls from Jameson.

Needless to say, I failed. Kind of like I am right now.

Last thing I want is to be desperate or bothersome. The clingy one who irritates him until breaking up is inevitable.

"He'll be here soon," Autumn says as she wipes down her booth and preps for her first session.

Her words hold truth, but every nerve ending under my skin is abuzz. Saturday night, Jameson asked if I wanted to go steady. It felt so 1950s. Sweet and heartfelt with a pinch of romantic. Had me swooning for hours. We texted briefly last night until he said he was with his mom. I didn't want to steal their time, so I told him I'd see him in the morning.

Now, it's morning, and he isn't here yet. Granted, he doesn't have an actual schedule, so morning could mean any time before noon. And the fact that I glance at the door every ten seconds...

What is wrong with me?

"Ugh," I huff out, more upset with my neediness than him not being here yet. "Why am I like this, Auti?"

She laughs. "Like what?"

I pin my fists to my hips and narrow my eyes at her. "A desperate lunatic." Ambling to her chair, I plop down and groan. "It hasn't been forty-eight hours and I'm checking my phone like he's a missing person and I'm waiting for a bronze alert." Autumn looks at me like I have three heads. "Well, I don't know what they call it when an adult is missing. Amber is for kids. Silver is for seniors. So I'm calling it bronze." I shrug and continue. "Why?" I drag the word out way too long with a heap of dramatic flair.

What does Autumn do? What does my best friend do? She laughs. Loud and clear and with too much gusto. *Some bestie she is.*

I slip off the chair and spin to face her, hands on my hips. "Best friends aren't supposed to give each other shit, Auti."

It takes her a moment, but she gets her laughter under control. "Is that so?"

I nod.

"Well, I remember you giving me plenty when things were new and messy with Jonas, so…" She makes a goofy face and then sticks out her tongue.

Just as I open my mouth to counter her comment, the bell over the door jingles. Plastering on my best welcoming smile, I turn on my heel to greet whoever walked in.

"Welcome to—" My throat goes dry as Jameson enters the shop, cups in carriers in both hands and a large bag tucked under his arm. "Oh, hey." I meet him halfway. "Let me help you."

I take one of the drink carriers from him, and we walk toward the reception desk. Autumn and Reznor join us and Iliana. "Not sure what everyone likes, but I brought coffee and bagels. I'll put the bagels in the back for whenever."

The shop doesn't open for another fifteen minutes, so we all dart to the break room and scarf down breakfast. A round of thanks is given to Jameson before everyone goes back to their workstations and the two of us go to the office.

Jameson follows me in and shuts the door behind him. The click of the latch hitting the strike plate is deafening. Each clunk of his boots on the hardwood is thunderous. And when he stops inches behind me and traces a finger down my forearm, I suck in a breath and freeze. My eyes fall shut as my mind drifts to the feel and taste of his lips on mine. I want to spin around. Want to know what he tastes like today.

But not here. Not in this office. Not where my actions could be misconstrued if someone waltzes in.

"Jameson," I croak. "We can't." His finger trails up to my elbow and I shake my head. "Not here."

His finger drops away and I instantly miss the blaze his touch sparks under my skin. But he doesn't leave me bereft for long. Warm lips meet the bare skin where my neck and shoulder connect. He touches me nowhere else, but I feel him everywhere. My pulse pounds a rhythm so vicious, he has to feel it beneath his lips.

Then his lips are gone. He doesn't step back, doesn't say a word. Part of me wants to lock the door and say fuck it. Part of me wants to spin around, palm his cheeks and lower his mouth to mine.

How long have I wanted this man? How long have I dated other men in the hopes they would make me forget him?

But I can't do this with him here. Selfish as I want to be in this very moment, I need to set boundaries. Work... we need to have rules.

He growls and takes a step back. I inhale for the first time in far too long. My feet are concrete boulders as I put one in front of the other and step around the desk. I don't want obstacles between us, but right now, I need something there to separate lust from reality.

Dropping down in the guest chair, he drags a hand through his beard. "God, I love being here with you every day." He shakes his head. "But if I make this too difficult" —he gestures between us with his other hand—"if it feels like I'm hindering things, tell me. Please."

Is it wrong for me to be happy over the fact that he thinks *he* is the only one that would disrupt the workday by us being together? He doesn't get it. Doesn't understand the gravity of what I feel for him. It may not be love —because I can't grasp the magnitude of love, not yet— but what I feel for Jameson… it has been brewing more years than not.

Sliding open the desk drawer, I pull out a pack of gum, take a piece and offer him one. He shakes his head. I drop the package back in the drawer, unwrap the cube and pop it in my mouth. Chew to soften the sweet, rubbery confection. Distract myself momentarily while I ponder how to navigate this—work, him, us—going forward. Jameson isn't going anywhere and neither am I.

"We need ground rules," I blurt out and nod. "We need to set clear boundaries of what's acceptable and not while we're working."

He relaxes in the chair further and spreads his legs wide. Like an addict, I watch his hand as it continues to stroke his beard. *God, I love the feel of that beard on my skin.* I shake my head briefly. *Knock it off, Penny. Focus.*

"Hmm." He eyes me a beat. "As awful as that sounds, you're probably right."

"Probably?" I cock my head and he chuckles.

"Mm-hmm." He straightens in the seat and reaches across the desk. I chew my gum with a vengeance as he inches closer and closer. Just when I think he is going to touch me again, he picks up the pad of paper and pen then resumes his previous position.

I am so screwed.

He scribbles on the pad, but I can't see what it says. Beneath the desk, my Chucks drum the hardwood. My nails tap the arms of the chair. And if it wouldn't be so damn obvious, my head would bob as I wait, wait, wait for him to finish writing whatever rules he thought of.

"Alright," he says, eyes trained on the paper. "Rules. Let's do this." His eyes lift from the page and lock on mine. Ready. Waiting.

My brows knit together as I point at the paper. "Did you write one down?"

He flips the pad around so I can see his tidy handwriting. On the top of the lined page, it says, *Penelope and Jameson's rules on how to not make out while at work.*

I look at him, then back at the page. I do this over and over and over. Nothing else is written on the page. And for a moment, all I think is how it reminds me of the early years, of pillow forts and rules on what you're allowed to do while in the fort. Then, without second thought, I laugh. I laugh loud and hard and until my stomach hurts and eyes water.

When my laughter settles and eyes clear, I peer across the desk to see the biggest smile on Jameson's face. A smile that gives me life and settles all worry. I love his smile. Always have. His smile is genuine and radiant and an accessory that adds to his appeal.

"You've always had the best laugh," he says.

"I'm quite fond of yours too." I blow a bubble with my gum then pop it. "Guess we should add some actual rules."

"If we want to get work done, yeah."

Over the next half hour, we shoot ideas back and forth. I veto some of his ideas—good morning kisses as well as lunchtime kisses—and he shoots down some of mine—office door open at all times and at least three feet separating us. Instead, we end up with a short list of basic office romance rules.

1. No kissing while working. If we leave for lunch, kissing is allowed.
2. No copping a feel or "inappropriate" touching while working.
3. Flirting is allowed, but nothing that gets "out of hand."
4. Everyone can know we're dating, but we won't flaunt it at work.
5. If no one is here or we're working late/after hours, rules 1-4 are null.

Rule number five was all Jameson. I fought it like this was junior year in debate class and Kyle Preston thought he knew more about women's rights than I did. Needless to say, Kyle Preston got buried with my rebuttal. Jameson, on the other hand, he wasn't taking no for an answer. Then he smiled and stroked his beard. What did I do? I caved.

Punk ass.

"Next time I run errands, I'm buying a frame for our rules," he says. He tears the page from the pad, folds it three times, then stuffs it in his pocket. "After the new furniture comes and the dust settles in here, I'll hang them on the wall."

Is he serious? Knowing Jameson, he will put it in the most obvious spot in the room. Hang it where every person that walks in will see it. Where they will read and laugh at the childish list of rules we had to make so we keep our hands and mouths off each other while at work.

"Maybe you should blow it up on an eleven-by-fourteen canvas," I tease.

He cocks a brow. "Don't tempt me. Now…" He rubs his hands together and lays his forearms on the desk. "We have calls to make. If you want to tackle the new hires, I'll call about the furniture and window."

I sit up straighter as my eyes gauge how serious he is. Not an ounce of humor or mischief lightens his smile or posture.

"Really? You'll add a window?"

"For you, yes. But also, I prefer natural light to fluo-rescents. Plus, maybe the chance of someone peeping in will keep me in line." He taps the pocket he stowed the rules in. "No guarantees, though."

While I call the six new faces of King of Hearts Ink— Sage, Chance, Frankie, Gage, Kennedy, and Ophelia— Jameson calls a friend who relays a few trustworthy window companies in the area. I suggest we ask my dad who to call for office furniture. If there is one thing George Singleton is an expert at, it is quality woodwork.

By lunch, each of the new staff is scheduled to come in later to pick up paperwork. Jameson has appointments scheduled for each window company to come out and give us an estimate. He wrote down addresses for two furniture galleries that said they have what we are looking for and, after lunch, we are headed to both. Since both of us will be crammed in the space, he said it was best for us to both go. To bounce ideas off each other or explain why certain pieces may not work in the space.

I shoulder my purse as we exit the office. Waving to Autumn and the guys, I stop at the front and hand Iliana envelopes for the new hires. "In case we don't make it back in time." Each envelope is labeled since not everyone requires the same paperwork.

The bell jingles as we step into the August heat. I dig in my purse for my sunglasses and slip them on as we round the building. The second we clear the windows, Jameson slips his hand in mine.

"Hey, mister."

He slides his own sunglasses into place, then flashes me a bright smile. "What? Technically, it's lunchtime." We reach my car and he steps into me, his other hand lifting to my cheek. "And if I want to touch"—the side of his finger strokes my jaw—"or kiss"—he drops his lips to mine and kisses me chastely—"my girl, I will." His finger paints a line down my throat. "Got it?" he asks, voice gruff.

Slowly, I nod. "Mm-hmm." I lick my lips, then swallow. "Got it."

"Good." He inches back and scans the length of my car. "Let's go. I've been dying to ride in this baby."

NINE

JAMESON

Jameson: Have dinner with me tonight.
Penny: How about you ask me nicely.

I walk up the next aisle in the office supply store. How many damn versions of staplers do they have? And pens... Jesus. I stared at the pen aisle—yes, the whole fucking aisle was pens—for a solid fifteen minutes. Gel. Ballpoint. Medium tip. Fine tip. Felt tip. Black. Blue. Every color known to exist in the spectrum. Sparkly. Shimmery. I grabbed a few boxes that looked like the ones Penny had in the office. You can never have too many pens.

Jameson: Penelope Jane, will you pretty please with sugar on top have dinner with me tonight?
Jameson: 🙏
Penny: Getting warmer.

Is it weird that her taunting is hot? The way she verbally teases me, eggs me on, smirks... damn, it is the best foreplay. Has me jonesing for more. Thinking of what I will say next. What she will say next.

So. Damn. Addicting.

Is it also weird that I never enjoyed foreplay until Penny?

Most of the women I dated in the past, the desire to feel that buildup, to feel the buzz in my veins and hum beneath my diaphragm, it wasn't there. The endless need for more. The insatiable hunger. I don't blame them. They were fun and beautiful and great. They just weren't who I was looking for. They weren't Penny.

Jameson: Penny, I would be honored with your presence for dinner tonight? *gets on knees in the stapler aisle*
Penny: Warmer 😢

An employee of the store is stocking the opposite side of the aisle with boxes of paper clips. I eye him for a minute and the best idea pops in my head. I wheel my buggy close to him.

"Excuse me, sir." He spins to face me, ready to help me find whatever office supplies I need. Little does he know, I am about to make this awkward. "This is an odd request, but can you do me the biggest, strangest favor?"

He sets the rest of the paper clips down and goes into full-on customer service mode. "Sure. What can I help you with?"

I open the camera app on my phone and hand him the phone. "Can you take a stupid picture? Of me, on my knees, on the floor." He looks at me like I might need medical attention. Perhaps I do. "It's a joke for my girlfriend."

Damn, I love the way girlfriend rolls off my tongue when Penny is said girl.

"Um…" He looks left then right. "I guess." He checks again to see if anyone else is nearby. Surely no one will fire the poor guy over this. "Just hurry."

I get down on my knees and lift my hands in a prayer position. The guy snaps a few pictures, then quickly hands me back my phone. "Thank you so much. I'll leave the best rating on the receipt survey." I read his name tag. "And add that you were extremely helpful, Don."

He nods and goes back to work, probably more than happy he doesn't have to deal with the weird guy anymore.

Jameson: Pretty, pretty please. With whipped cream and jimmies and cherries.
Jameson: *photo delivered*
Penny: Oh. My. Gawd. 🙈 You made someone take a picture of you begging in the store?!
Jameson: Maybe 😇
Penny: Yes, Jameson. I'll have dinner with you.

Halle-fucking-lujah!

When it comes to Penny, I am obviously not above

groveling or taking strange photos in public. Her reaction is worth it. Every. Single. Time.

Jameson: See you at 6.

I send her my address and take a deep breath. Then, I frolic through the rest of the aisles like the parents in commercials for back-to-school time, tossing random shit the shop probably doesn't need in the cart. 'Cause who cares… Penny will be at my house tonight.

K♥
Q♥

Cooking a meal has never intimidated me. In fact, most days I love standing at the stove and tossing random ingredients in a pan. Concocting new meals on a whim. Mom taught me the basics and said, "There're no rules in cooking, Jameson. Except for baking. Follow the rules when baking." Some of my favorite dishes came to life by not following recipes.

Cooking has never intimidated me… until now.

I stare in the pantry, scan the rice and quinoa and pasta. Get lost in the canned beans and bread crumbs and jarred herbs. Panic when I reach the flour and sugar and cornmeal with still no plan for dinner.

Pulling my phone from my back pocket, I unlock it, open my call history and tap on the first name. My fingers tap the counter as the phone rings in my ear once, twice.

"Hey, sweetheart," Mom answers in the tone that melts my heart. "Two calls in one day. You know how to make a lady feel special."

"Hey, Ma. I need help."

Something rustles in the background. "Everything okay, Jameson?" Concern laces her voice and I want to smack myself for not choosing my words better.

"Yeah. Sorry. Didn't mean to scare you." I take a deep breath. "Uh... I invited a woman over for dinner and it seems I suddenly forgot what to do in the kitchen."

"Do I know this woman?" Curiosity floats between her words as she speaks.

Mom does know Penny. Seeing as Enzo and I were together more often than not during our teen years, Mom had been to their house. She and Dad befriended Greta and George Singleton. We mingled at holiday parties with them. Joined them for scary movie marathons with pizza and popcorn and mounds of sugar.

Their family and ours... we were tight.

Which is probably the reason I am so damn nervous about telling her. Mom has known Penny for years. Although she may not know as much now as she once did. Mom and Greta still chatted on occasion, but I doubt conversations about "the kids" came up as often as it once did. Us kids are in our thirties now. Our mothers probably have better things to gab about than us.

"Actually, yes."

The line goes silent a moment. I open my mouth to ask if she heard me, but she cuts me off. "Are you going to tell me who?" Light laughter fills the line. "Or is this some game where I guess?"

Why, why, why am I so nervous?

Mom has always loved Penny. Thought of her like a daughter. Blathered on about how cute she was in her polka-dot dresses and black Mary Janes.

But I doubt Mom has seen her in the last several years. Not as if Penny hangs out at home while our mothers catch up. Although Penny is the same woman I knew years ago, she has changed so much. Become more herself. Bolder. Vibrant. Alluring.

"I, uh…" *Just spit it out already.* "I started seeing Penny," I say in a rush.

Once again, the line falls silent. Maybe I should have had this call over FaceTime. At least I would have some idea of what Mom is thinking versus waiting impatiently for a response.

"Hmm," she hums. *What the hell does that mean? Hmm.* Before I get the chance to ask, she continues. "Well, can't say I'm surprised."

Wait. What? "I'm sorry?" I ask as if I misunderstood her.

"You and Penelope dating, it doesn't surprise me."

"It doesn't?"

Light laughter floats through the line. "No, sweetheart. Honestly, I thought it would've happened sooner."

"Really?"

The volume of her laughter kicks up a notch. "Greta and I both thought so. I mean, the way you two looked at each other when the other wasn't paying attention… the affection you shared was blatantly obvious."

My eyes fall shut as I run a hand down my face and clutch my chin. Yes, I spent several minutes each day with my eyes on Penny when we were younger. But I didn't realize she did the same. Nor did I realize our parents witnessed the exchanges.

"Um… okay." My hand falls away as my eyes pop open. The pantry comes back into view and I remember why this awkward call is happening in the first place. I shake off my wayward thoughts and get back on track. "Back to why I called."

"You need help figuring out what to cook," she says, more as a statement than a question.

"Yes." I glance at the stove and lose focus. "I'd like to cook her something nice for dinner, but every time I look in the pantry, the ideas go out the window."

For the next ten minutes, Mom asks questions about what I have on hand. Minute by minute, she helps narrow down what to cook and what to avoid. Penny would probably be happy eating burgers and fries. One night, I will put that on the menu. Tonight though, I want to cook a nice meal. Nothing fancy. Just something she will appreciate. A dish that will make her want me to cook for her more often.

With all the ingredients on the counter, Mom and I chat another minute or two as I fetch pots and pans from the cabinet.

"No need to be nervous, Jameson. You've known Penny a long time."

I grab the olive oil and rosemary. "Maybe that's exactly *why* I am nervous." My hand reaches for the head of garlic on the counter. "What if I mess this up? This is Penny, Mom. Not some random woman." I shake my head. "I can't mess things up with her."

"Oh, sweetheart." Her voice softens on the other end. "You would never hurt her. Not on purpose." She sounds so matter of fact. "Just be yourself. You don't need to impress her with extravagant meals and flashy dates." She pauses for a beat. "The attraction is already there. For both of you. This is the time to get to know each other as adults. Learn about the parts you've missed over the years. Explore life together."

Mom always knows what to say. Knows how to reassure me when life feels wobbly.

Although a gap exists in the time we have known each other, I do know Penny. What makes her smile and laugh. What gets under her skin and makes her your worst nightmare. And what makes her soft and submissive and irresistible. More than anything, I want to make up for the missed years with her. Fill in the gaps with new memories. Unforgettable memories. Of her and me and the irrefutable connection we share.

"Thanks, Mom." I fetch the cutting board and a knife. "For everything. I should go. She'll be here in…" I check the time on the stove. "Shit, a little over an hour."

"Breathe, sweetheart. Everything will be fine. I love you."

"Love you, too."

The call disconnects, and I shove my phone in my pocket then get to work on dinner.

No need to panic. This is Penny. You know *Penny. Breathe. Everything is fine.*

God, I hope so.

TEN

PENNY

From the driver's seat, eyes wide, I stare at Jameson's house. Can this even be classified as a house? Jesus. Looks like ten people could live here. Far as I know, Jameson lives alone.

So why the ostentatious house? And where the hell did he get money for something this flashy? I may have missed several years of his life, but Enzo would have mentioned his best friend buying a million-dollar home on the beach.

With a deep breath filling my lungs, I yank on the handle and swing the car door open. Step out and smooth my dress down my thighs. Shoulder my purse, shut the door and start the trek to the larger-than-life house. The heels of my shoes clap against the sand-colored pavers as I slowly approach double oak doors.

Two steps away from reaching the front door, it swings open and my belly instantly warms as Jameson welcomes me with the biggest smile.

Over the years, I have seen this man smile countless times. Have memorized each one and earmarked my favorites. This smile is new. Like an all-consuming hug that heats your blood and warms your bones.

I love this smile. Mark it as my new favorite.

"Hey, Pen." He steps to the side and holds the door open wider. "Come in."

Stepping past him, my eyes dart around the space. Tall ceilings, polished oak, marble, and so many windows. The foyer feels bigger than the living room in my apartment. Not a speck of dust in sight. Every surface sparkles more than my Cadillac after a wax job.

It's beautiful and bright and grandiose. But it doesn't feel like Jameson. Not in the slightest.

I picture him in a home more quaint. Three bedrooms, a living room big enough to comfortably seat guests, and a kitchen with lots of counter space for gatherings. A covered patio in an expansive backyard. A palette of cream and black and an array of browns.

When I think of Jameson, warmth floods my veins.

This house… it feels cold and empty and everything Jameson is not.

He closes the door, slips his hand in mine and walks us through the living and dining rooms until we reach the kitchen. My feet skid to a halt.

"Jesus," I whisper in shock.

Beside me, Jameson laughs. "Isn't it a bit much?"

As we enter the open kitchen, I survey every surface and scrunch my brows. "Kind of a weird thing to say about your own house."

Spinning around, he takes my other hand in his, steps into me and smiles. Every part of him consumes every part of me in this moment. The rich woodsy scent of his cologne. The heat from his body as he inches closer. The strength of his hold. And the way his eyes drop to my lips, I read his message loud and clear.

I push up on my toes and bring my lips to his. Kiss him chastely—once, twice—until one of his hands drops mine, glides up the column of my throat to the nape of my neck and locks me in place. Warm and wet and inviting, the tip of his tongue strokes the seam of my lips. Begs me to let him in. I part my lips. Invite him in. Stroke his tongue with mine and revel in the groan that rumbles in his throat.

God, he tastes good. Savory and indulgent. Sweet and sinful. The type of sin made only for me.

Far too soon, he breaks the kiss. If I had my wits about me, I might be embarrassed by my panting. Might care about the heat staining my cheeks. But that ship sailed on our date night when he kissed me in public and stole every coherent thought I owned.

Jameson presses his forehead to mine, frames my face with his palms. "God, I love kissing you." I hum and he leans in for another taste, this one brief. Too brief as he straightens his spine and his hands fall away. "This isn't my house. Belongs to a friend from college. He lives in Northern California most of the year, but isn't a fan of snow."

A wave of confusion crashes against me as I look around the house. It looks more lived in than if he were just keeping an eye on it. Small pieces of him in the kitchen and living room. Framed photos of him and his parents, him and Enzo, and a few others I don't know. A stack of tattoo magazines on the coffee table beneath a paperback appears well loved. A small rosemary and basil plant on the window ledge in the kitchen. Fresh lisianthus flowers in various shades of pink and white.

The house doesn't feel like Jameson, but it feels lived in.

"Are you staying here?" I ask as he kisses my hand before relinquishing it.

"Temporarily. Drink?" He opens the fridge and reaches for a pitcher.

"Please."

Fetching glasses from the cupboard, he pours us each water with citrus and cucumber slices. *Fancy.* He hands me a glass, puts the pitcher back and moves toward the stove. My eyes follow his every step. Rake over his broad shoulders as they stretch the black cotton of his T-shirt. Down his spine to the plump curves of his…

Jameson laughs and my eyes dart north. His eyes peek at me over his shoulder. A shit-eating grin splits his face in half. In point-five seconds, my face flames.

Yes, we are officially dating. Yes, I have felt every inch of my body pressed to his. But damn, I did not want to be caught ogling him. Did not want to get caught staring at his ass while he cooks dinner. It was a private moment. One I rather enjoyed. One I will conjure in the future as I lie in bed, close my eyes and drift off.

He sets down the wooden spoon, turns off the burner,

and pulls a pan out of the oven. He futzes with the foil covering the pan as I sip my water. And just when I think he won't say anything, just when I think he's moved on and will plate dinner, he pivots and saunters over to me on the opposite side of the kitchen island. Grabs one of my hips, then the other. Hauls me forward until my breasts graze his chest. He dips his head, trails his nose up the side of my neck, and inhales my skin until he reaches my ear.

Who needs oxygen? This girl, that's who.

"Penelope Jane," he purrs in my ear. "Were you checking out my butt?"

I want to laugh. Want to blow off the moment as a joke. Slap the air and play off my actions.

But there isn't a chance in hell of that happening. Not with Jameson breathing down my neck. Literally. At the rate this is going, dinner will be cold by the time we sit down to eat. Not that I care.

I bite my lower lip and shrug. "Maybe." No sense in denying it, not when he caught me in the act.

He hums against my skin, his breath hot beneath my ear, and my eyes fall shut. My hands grip the cotton of his shirt. Fist the material over his abdomen. Tug him closer until every inch of us is connected.

"Could kiss you all night," he says, voice gruff. "But I want to take my time with you, Pen." His fingers bruise my hips. "Navigate this, us, slowly." He presses his lips to the skin beneath my ear. "I've wanted this for so long." He inches back until our eyes meet. "I want to do this right."

Well, damn.

Speechless, I nod. "Me too."

A soft smile peeks through his facial hair before he kisses my forehead. I close my eyes and breathe deeply until he pulls away.

He rounds the island and moves toward the stove. Dips a finger in one pot, then sucks it clean and nods. He fetches plates from a cabinet and portions out dinner. And he does it all with such ease.

As I track his every move, the only thought in my head is... *how did I not know Jameson was a romantic?*

Has he done this for every woman he dated? Or is this domestic version of the punk I knew years ago new? I would like to think Jameson doesn't cook dinner for just anyone. That he reserves this side of himself for people close to him. People who matter. Family and loved ones.

He carries the plates to the dining room table then returns for his drink. He takes my hand and walks me to the table. Pulls out my chair and scoots it back after I am seated. Sits beside me, not across from me, probably because this table is equally as grandiose as the house. Sitting on opposite sides would put too much space between us. Something neither of us wants tonight.

"This looks and smells amazing."

"Thank you."

Over dinner, Jameson tells me about the friend, Ricardo, who owns this house. Jameson met Ricardo during his second year in college. Ricardo isn't the type to party all night and Jameson found it somewhat refreshing. When his dormmates wanted to stay up all hours and party until sunrise, Jameson hung out with Ricardo. Camped on his couch every once in a while.

While Jameson recants his college years, I give him every ounce of my attention. Listen to the stories about pranks he pulled on others and the pranks they did to him. Listen to the struggles he incurred in his last year and his fear of not graduating. More than anything, I listen to how much those years shaped the man in front of me.

Jameson is still the guy I knew years ago. Handsome and loyal and genuine. He doesn't skirt around what he wants. Doesn't leave anything to chance. Dives in headfirst.

But part of him has changed. Not in the physical sense —unless you count how thick his muscles are now. Jameson has always been kind. Gentle, even. Now, though, he seems softer around the edges. Affectionate on a level I haven't seen from him.

Perhaps it is because I never saw this side of him. The side he gives to a companion or lover.

Or perhaps something happened and changed his outlook. Took his perspective and reshaped it into something new and significant and crucial.

"So where do you live when you're not shacking up in this swanky place?"

"Been house hunting without much success. Usually I stay with Mom. How grown up of me, right?" He chuckles, then sips his water.

"How are your parents? I haven't seen them in so long." Jameson freezes and his face pales. *What did I say?* I drop my fork then clutch his face in my hands and tilt his head so our eyes meet. "What's wrong?"

Tears flood his eyes as he stares back. His teeth hold his lips prisoner as he works his jaw back and forth. He does his best to not let it show, but I feel his body quake beneath my hands. A slight shake of his head as if what I am asking is unbelievable.

"You don't know," he mutters.

My thumbs stroke his cheeks. "Don't know what?"

The first tear falls and I want to swipe it away, but don't move an inch. If what I said brought Jameson to tears, whatever happened must be bad.

"My dad." He licks his lips and swallows as the next tear slides down his cheek. "He… he…" His eyes fall shut, and I hate that this hurts him so much. That he feels the need to hide himself before he confesses his pain to me. Then his eyes pop open and hold mine. "He died." My eyes widen as I go stock-still. "Last year. From pneumonia."

"Oh my…" My throat goes dry as I digest his words. *Why did no one tell me this?* I twist to face him, wrap my arms around his neck and hug him tightly. "Jameson, I'm sorry. I-I didn't know." Curse my family for not relaying such a critical piece of information. I may not have seen Jameson or his family for years, but I still cared. And we had all been so close for so many years. "God, I'm so sorry."

Time moves, but we don't. I hold Jameson in my arms as he hugs me with unparalleled ferocity. Wetness hits my shoulders, but he doesn't sob or wail. He simply lets the tears fall. Lets another dose of his pain go and allows me to comfort him.

I hate that I didn't know. But as contradictory as it sounds, I like that I heard the news from Jameson. That he shared this life update while it is just him and me and no one to shape either of our reactions.

He loosens his hold around my waist. Kisses my shoulder before swiping a hand over his cheeks. "Sorry I took the evening from happy to sad in no time."

My hands frame his face as I lift his chin. "No, Jameson." I shake my head for emphasis. "Thank you for telling me. Sucks I didn't know, but I'm glad I found out from you." I lean in and kiss his tearstained cheeks. "How's your mom?"

As we clear the table, Jameson tells me how Lorraine Kingsley has moved on since Harold passed. The hysterics and denial. The endless stream of tears for weeks. And the wake-up call she had after watching her husband leave at such an early age. Now, she teaches senior exercise classes at the city rec center. Has found comfort with friends and peace within the new life she has been handed.

Although Harold's passing was difficult for them both, he said they both learned to not take anything in life for granted. You just never know what happens next.

Couldn't agree more.

Jameson stows the last of the dishes in the dishwasher and starts the load. Then he opens a cabinet on the island and retrieves a serving platter. A charcuterie board, but not just any charcuterie board. Nope. This one is loaded with sweets.

I stare down at the artful display of Twizzlers and M&M's, Skittles and Butterfinger bars, Mike and Ikes and Baby Ruths. Let's not forget the Nutter Butters and Vienna Fingers. It takes me a moment to process what I see. That this man made a dessert platter designed specifically with me in mind. A man who remembers my sweet tooth and need for variety.

"This is…" I peer up at him and forget to breathe for a beat. My favorite smile is back in place. *Jameson Kingsley is beyond perfect.* "This is the most incredible gift ever." I scan the display again. "Where's yours?" I tease and we both crack up.

And then, Jameson escorts me to the couch. We toss a throw blanket over our legs, eat tons of sugar and stream a random show neither of us know. When I wake up hours later, Jameson is carrying me down a hallway. I don't worry about sleeping arrangements or clothes or work in the morning. Instead, I hug him tighter. Inhale his scent. And fall back asleep in Jameson's arms.

ELEVEN

JAMESON

Mumbled words stir me from sleep, and I hug Penny closer to my side. I may be sweating two days' worth of calories with her limbs draped over my body, but there is no way in hell I am peeling her off.

"Pick up your socks," she grumbles in her sleep.

I bite my tongue and fight off the laughter begging to spill from my chest. All the years I have known Penny, learning she talks in her sleep is a fun little surprise. A trait I plan to tease her about.

Glancing at the alarm clock, I note we need to get up in the next fifteen minutes. Penny doesn't have another set of clothes and we should both get to work at a decent time.

Managing the tattoo shop isn't quite the same as a retail store or corporate business. We don't have to punch time cards. Don't have daily conference calls. Nor do we have a true, set schedule. Yes, we have a list of tasks to do daily, weekly, monthly, etc. But there is no one to hover

over us, no one to shake a finger at us for not accomplishing said tasks by a certain hour.

Owning the shop is a labor of love. The least stressful job I've had over the years. Part of that is because it came with good bones. A solid foundation because of the previous owner and close-knit team.

I got lucky with this shop. Damn lucky. In more ways than one.

Penny's hand drifts up my chest, my neck, and into my hair. I toy with the length of her strands as my eyes roll back at her touch. Even in sleep, her touch is perfection. Fire in my veins and comfort to my soul. Like coming home after a long journey alone.

I never want this moment to end. Penny tucked into my side. Breath warm on my neck. Leg draped over my hips. Fingers in my hair while her nails graze my scalp. Her fruity scent on my sheets and mumbled words in my ears.

Beneath the sheet, my free hand caresses her thigh just above the knee. My arm around her back hugs her incrementally tighter. I inhale deeply and live in the moment for three more breaths before I break the bliss bubble.

"Pen," I whisper. She groans against my neck, and I allow my slight chuckle to shake my frame. "Sweets, we need to get up."

Another groan rumbles through her, this one a little louder. "I don't wanna." Her limbs tighten their hold on me. "Did you just call me Sweets?"

I turn my head a fraction and press my lips to her forehead. "Seems fitting." Not just for her addiction to all things sugary, but also because I have been sweet on this woman for years.

Her nails scrape my scalp as her lips trail up my neck. A low growl builds in my chest as I secure my grip on her. My fingers drift higher on her thigh and up her spine. With each kiss of her lips on my skin, my heart shifts into the next gear. My pulse pounding faster, harder.

When she reaches the angle of my jaw, she bares her teeth. Grazes the skin through my beard and sinks in slightly.

In a blink, I roll her onto her back. Hover inches above her. Pin her hands on either side of her face while my hips pin hers to the mattress. Stare down at her and note the shift in her green eyes. The bolder shade in her usually pale irises.

The way she stares back has me ravenous. Makes me never want to leave this bed. Makes me want to hold her captive until we have both had our fill. Not that I think either of us will ever have our fill.

I slam my mouth down on hers. Kiss her slow and deep and hard. Kiss her fast and hungry. No kiss will make up for the countless ones I wanted to give her over the years, but that won't stop me from trying. Not only will I make up for those lost opportunities, I plan to kiss this woman every day for the rest of our lives.

I release her hands, cup her cheek with one while the other drifts lower to her hip. Her hands go to either side of my waist before trailing up the sides of my spine. Her legs wrapping around my waist. Although she is fully dressed and I have on a pair of sweats, I have never felt more naked. More exposed and open.

She tastes sweet on my tongue as her curves mold perfectly against my body. Her hungry moans flood my ears while her scent consumes the air. She is everywhere, everything. Yet, I need more of her. Want more.

But it will have to wait. Not just because we need to get up and go to work, but because I want to take my time with Penny. Savor every taste of her skin and tongue and lips. Relish every one of her curves beneath my hands. Revel in the sight of her each day I have her on my arm. Take pleasure in the fall—mine and hers.

Against every testosterone-laden cell in my body, I break the kiss. Press my forehead to hers and drop one last peck. Smile as she groans in disappointment.

"We should get up."

Her hands slip down to the waistband of my sweats, pause briefly before her fingers dance over my flesh from spine to hip. I close my eyes and stop breathing.

"We should, but…" Her breath warm on my lips.

I drop a swift kiss on her lips. Growl as she tries to hold me to her. Break the kiss and roll off her before rising from the bed. When I glance back to the bed, Penny has her bottom lip pushed out. And fuck me… there is no chance in hell of me hiding what the sight does to me, to my body.

"You're trouble, Penelope Singleton."

Moving to her hands and knees, she crawls toward me. A woman on a mission. A woman determined to make me fall at her feet. Metaphorically speaking, I fell long ago.

"Never claimed otherwise," she taunts. She reaches me, eyes locked on the apparent bulge beneath my sweats before rising up on her knees. "Don't you want to get in trouble with me?"

"God, yes." I frame her face with my hands. Kiss her madly. "But we have time. Plenty of time."

Her bottom lip pops out again, and I lean in to nip at it. "Guess you're right," she acquiesces. Her butt hits the mattress. "Fine." She dramatically drags out the word. "Let's go to work."

Dramatics still in full effect, she slides off the mattress and ambles toward the door. Before she steps out of reach, I take her hand in mine, haul her to my chest and kiss the hell out of her. I hate that she has to leave. That she has to walk out the front door, drive away from the house and go back to her apartment to dress for work.

We may be in the early stages of our romantic relationship, but that little fact doesn't halt the idea of cohabitating with Penny from popping in my head. Because damn, how incredible it would be to wake up with her every morning. To see her before the day begins, hair wild and face free of makeup.

But it's too soon.

I hate that she has to leave, but I won't scare her by asking for more. Yet.

"See you soon."

Every night over the last two weeks, Penny and I have slept in the same bed. More in hers than the bed I occupy at Ricardo's place. Surrounded by her belongings, her smell, being in her bed and space, feels more like home.

Our nights together haven't evolved past extreme make-out sessions and heavy petting, which I am more than okay with. I hadn't lied when I told Penny I want to go slow. That I want to take my time. In a world where too many things are rushed nowadays, the best moments and experiences come from that slow build. From the anticipation of how it will all unfold. The picture we paint in our minds on just how great it will be when it finally happens.

Day by day, Penny opens herself more. Shows me pieces of her I missed in the years we saw little of each other. Exposes her heart, one layer at a time.

And I grant her the same in return.

For years, infatuation filled my veins at the thought of Penny. But I shoved it down. Buried it deep in the recesses of my mind. Ignored my attraction for her and did everything to wipe my best friend's little sister from my wandering thoughts.

Now, though… there is no need to hide. Not how I feel or what I want.

What I want is Penny. All of her. Always.

Giggles come from the end of the hall and echo into the living room, the sound barely audible over the television. Penny groans, then leans forward, grabs the remote, and cranks the volume higher. Bounces her knee as she looks down the hall every few seconds.

Roommates have as many pitfalls as they do perks. Yeah, it's great to cut the financial burdens of living solo. It's great to have someone to chat with on days off, to build a greater relationship. To call them family. But just like family, roommates can be annoying as hell. Unhygienic and loud. Eating and drinking the last of something and not replenishing it. Or worse, leaving barely any in the container and not mentioning the need for more. Then, there is the occasional night guest. Yes, I fit into this category, but I respect the fact Penny has a roommate. I keep the volume to a minimum, pick up after myself and respect Rex's space.

Wish I could say the same about the woman he brought home for the third night this week.

"Argh," Penny groans as laughter sounds over the television again.

I tuck a lock of hair behind Penny's ear and kiss her temple. "We can head out. Go to Ricardo's for the night."

She hums. "Tempting." Her fingers toy with the hem of my shirt. Fist the cotton lightly and tug. "So tempting."

I lift a hand to her chin and tip it up until our eyes lock. "Then say yes." I drop a chaste kiss to her lips.

Before I pull back from the kiss, her hand comes to the nape of my neck and she brings my lips back to hers. The kiss is slow and sweet for one, two, three passes. Then she nips at my bottom lip. Sucks it between hers. Swallows my moan as she deepens the kiss.

She shifts beside me, her leg going over both of mine before she straddles my lap and frames my face in her hands. The television show forgotten as she hauls me impossibly closer, presses her breasts to my chest, and rocks her hips over the bulge beneath my zipper.

"Let's go, Pen," I mutter as her lips trail down my neck. I fist her hips with a bruising grip.

Her teeth nip the skin where my shoulder and neck meet. "Yes." She kisses the same spot and lifts her gaze to mine. "Let's go."

TWELVE

PENNY

PURE BLISS.

Jameson's hands snake around my bare waist from behind. His lips on my neck as I lean into him and drop my head on his shoulder. His chest vibrates against my spine as my fingers knead his thighs.

"Damn, you feel incredible in my arms."

My thighs clamp together at his words. At the feel of him behind me, against me, around me. I want more. *Need* more.

I spin in his arms and straddle his lap. Water splashes from the hot tub over the edge as I eliminate all space between us. As I comb my fingers through his hair and bring my lips to his. As I rock my hips over his, a thin layer of swimwear between us, and kiss the hell out of him.

For weeks, it has been like this. Fiery and greedy and obsessive. But neither of us has pushed for more. Neither of us has made the first move to eliminate barriers. To move past intense make-out sessions with full on groping through clothes.

Jameson said he wanted to take things slow. Wanted us to not rush our relationship. Much as I hated the idea two months ago, I am glad we set this pace. Glad we spent time learning the new us.

Now, though… I am ready for more. Ready for the next step.

"Jameson," I breathe out. My hand trails down his midline, his abdomen, to the hem of his board shorts. I tug at the strings and he gasps. I kiss along his jaw and stop at his ear. "I want you." My fingers deftly untie the strings of his shorts before my hand inches beneath the fabric. "I need you."

His fingers bruise my hips as a groan spills from his lips. "Fuck." The word a whisper, a plea, a cry for mercy and more.

Not a breath passes before we exit the hot tub. My legs circle his waist and my hands fist his hair. His stride confident and steady and swift as we move through the house and enter the bedroom. Then I fly through the air, a burst of thrill in my veins and laughter on my tongue. Jameson crawls up the mattress until all I see is him.

"You sure?" he asks, his face never more serious.

I bring a hand to his cheek, stroke the scruffy line of his jaw and watch as he leans into my touch. "Yes," I whisper. "Never been more sure."

His mouth claims mine in the sweetest, most heady kiss. His hands roam the curves of my hips, my breasts, my ass. Fire ignites beneath my skin as his fingers scrape and knead and caress my flesh. My heart beats a vicious rhythm against my rib cage as my breath comes faster and faster. A faint hum builds low in my abdomen, begging for more.

My back bows off the bed and Jameson unfastens my bikini top. His hand glides down my spine until it reaches my lower back and lifts my hips. He rocks into me, and our moans fill the room. I toss the material to the floor before reaching for his shorts. We fumble as I work his shorts down his thighs and he tugs at my bottoms.

And then we bare every part of ourselves to each other. Expose our flesh as well as our hearts. In this moment, I have never felt more naked in my life. Never more vulnerable and anxious. But also never more at ease and safe.

Jameson's eyes never leave mine. Not to ogle my breasts or stare where our hips connect. And damn, his eyes have never been this blue. This piercing. This compelling.

I wrap him in my arms and hug him close. Bring his lips to mine. Kiss him as our bodies connect in a new way.

The kiss breaks as Jameson reaches for the nightstand and opens the top drawer. Without looking, he searches the drawer and retrieves a condom. His lips take mine again. Kiss me senseless and express every emotion neither of us has said aloud.

He tears the wrapper open and rolls on the condom. Just when I think he will rock his hips forward, he kisses his way down my body. Kisses his way to one breast—growls when he spots the barbell—then the other. He trails kisses down my abdomen until he reaches the small patch of curls.

And then he is there. Between my thighs. Licking my most sensitive place. Tasting me in the most intimate way. Moaning as his arms wrap around my thighs, he yanks me closer than close and devours me like I am his first real meal.

I fist his hair. Grind my center against his insatiable mouth. Bow my back off the bed as my moan fills the room. He wraps my clit with his lips and sucks, hard and fast and determined. My grip tightens on his hair. Tugs until he moans and vibrates my sensitive flesh. Heat builds in my chest and crawls up my neck, my cheeks. My eyes slam shut as light flashes behind my lids.

Jameson licks up my center and moans. "Fuck, you're sweet on my tongue."

I release his hair as my pulse whooshes in my ears. Not a beat passes before Jameson crawls up my body and positions his cock at my entrance. His mouth captures mine in a slow, seductive kiss. The taste of my orgasm on his tongue adds a new dose of adrenaline to my blood-stream. Makes me high—on him, on us.

He breaks the kiss, then hovers motionless above me. My eyes open and lock with his. Lock on to the icy-blue orbs that say more than his lips ever will. In them, I see the love this man has for me. Has had for me for longer than either of us will admit aloud.

For the first time, I don't fear it. Don't fear the deep emotional connection of another. The most intimate and beautiful connection. For the first time, I want nothing more. I crave it more than my next breath, the next beat of my heart.

Knuckles lightly brush my cheekbone before Jameson rocks his hips forward and fills me fully. His jaw falls lax while his eyes roll back a beat. My hands roam his back until they reach the firm muscles of his glutes. Eyes back on mine, our bodies move in tandem. Find a rhythm new to us. I can't look away. Refuse to miss a second of his pleasure as he gives me mine.

And fuck me if this is not the most erotic moment of my life. Watching Jameson as he pants for oxygen. As his pulse throbs in his neck. As his skin grows flush and his irises morph into a darker shade of blue.

It is too much and not enough. His hot breath on my skin. Our moans vibrating the walls. The scent of our arousal in the air. Our skin slapping and fingers bruising.

The same familiar heat builds in my chest. It spreads like a forest fire, dropping low in my belly, crawling up my neck and cheeks. Building. Burning. Devouring. My moans switch to whimpers as he pistons his hips faster. As he hits that spot deep inside me again and again.

"Jameson." His name a litany on my tongue. An endless whisper in the night. My first breath of oxygen and true beat of my heart.

I let go and stop breathing for a beat. Jameson's lips crash to mine as his hips work faster. Then his hips stutter, his body jerking as he fills me with his release. As he breathes my name against my lips.

As our bodies calm and reality settles around us,

Jameson presses his forehead to mine. Kisses the tip of my nose as he twirls a lock of my hair with his finger.

"I love you, Penelope Singleton."

My body goes rigid. Freezes without warning. I don't know why, but hearing the words aloud… I shut down. Although I mentally and emotionally reciprocate one hundred percent, my physical self is on a different page.

"I…" My eyes dart between his as an overwhelming tightness squeezes my chest. "I…"

Fuck.

THIRTEEN

JAMESON

FUCK.

Did I seriously just fuck this up with Penny? Did I open my big-ass mouth and drop the L-bomb?

Fuck, fuck, fuck.

I see it in her eyes. The crippling anxiety of saying the wrong thing after I told her I loved her. It isn't a lie. But hell, it is too damn soon to declare such emotions. At least it is too early for her.

"Penny, I…"

I close my eyes, take a deep breath and pull out of her. Dropping my back on the mattress, I drape a hand over my eyes and gather my thoughts. I don't regret how I feel. More than anything, I regret speaking too soon. I regret saying something she isn't ready to hear. Because I know she feels it. The way she looks at me, I just know.

After another deep breath, I trudge forward. Best to lay all my cards on the table now. Rolling onto my side, I wait until she turns her head and looks me in the eye.

"Is it too soon to confess how I feel?" I shrug. "Probably. But it doesn't change the fact that I do love you." She swallows as her eyes dart between mine. I toy with a lock of her hair before tucking it behind her ear. "Love is scary as hell, Pen. But after losing my dad, I don't hold back like I once did. I don't bottle up what I feel. Not anymore." My finger traces the line of her jaw. "I didn't intend to say that just now." I laugh. "Actually wanted it to be in a more romantic setting. A nice dinner and night out." The corners of her lips curve up in a slight smile. This is good. "Pen, you make me feel so much here." I press the heel of my palm to my sternum. "It scares me to death, but also brings me to life."

Her hand cups my jaw, her thumb stroking my cheek as her fingers scrape through my beard. Without a word, she leans forward and presses her lips to mine. Kisses me sweeter than any time previous. I moan against her lips. Melt into her touch. Bask in the gentle intimacy of her and me and premature confessions.

She breaks the kiss, inches back and holds my gaze. Her fingers still stroking my cheek and jaw. Slowly, she starts to nod. The movement almost imperceptible, but I see it.

"Love is scary." She swallows and runs her thumb over my cheekbone. "God, is it ever." Her hand drifts higher. Her fingers combing through my hair. "And although it wasn't quite like this, I loved you a long time ago."

My brows pinch at the middle as my eyes search hers for more answers. "Then why did you freeze?"

She leans in and places a chaste kiss on my lips.

"When you've loved someone as long as I have you, but neither of us has been here, in the place where confessions flow freely, it's foreign. Unfamiliar territory." One of her shoulders rises and falls. "I can't tell you how many times I dreamed of us feeling the same way. How many times I dreamed of hearing you say that you loved me." Her tongue darts out and wets her lips before she swallows. "But when you actually said the words… it stunned me."

She is not freaked out. She is not deterred by the love bomb. *Thank fuck.*

"I'd rather stun you than chase you off."

Had I scared Penny away, God… I'd have been kicking myself in the ass for years. Probably pulling out all the stops to get her back. On my knees—again—embarrassing myself with the hopes of having her in my arms once more.

But I didn't frighten her. I shocked her.

By spilling my heart prematurely, I opened the door to the possibility of something incredible. With her. Now that I have her, now that I am privy to her reciprocal affection, a form of love we have both felt for years, I want to throw another bomb in the mix. Might as well get them all out in one shot.

Whoever listens to my internal ramblings, please let her say yes.

My knuckles graze her cheek before I lean in and kiss her soft lips. When our eyes meet, her body goes lax, sighing with contentment. What I say next may add to that happiness or steal it completely. Fingers crossed it is the former.

"Pen..." I lick my lips, then swallow past the lump building in my throat. Soft fingers caress my bearded jaw. For two breaths, I close my eyes and bask in the fire it sparks in the center of my chest. When I open my eyes and find her watching me, I bite the bullet and speak my heart. "I'd like us to live together."

Her fingers stop their gentle strokes as her eyes lose focus. A comatose look washes over her face. Has she taken a breath since the words left my lips? I can't be certain. As freaked out as I thought she was by my love confession, this may be the final straw.

What the hell was I thinking?

If telling her I love her felt like it was far too soon, why the hell did I follow it up with the suggestion of living together? Because I am a goddamn idiot, that is why.

I mentally slap myself as I watch Penny slip into a silent panic attack. *Please say something.* If only I could hear the thoughts flitting through her mind. If only I knew where her head is at.

Did I fuck this up? Did I break something that was on wobbly ground only minutes ago?

"Pen?" My eyes dart between hers in search of clues, but she has them on lockdown. "Please say something. I'm losing my shit here."

Then her fingers, still on my jaw, start to move again. Small soft strokes as she blinks away the fog. Although she doesn't look as if she will throw the idea in the garbage, there is no indication she likes the notion of us cohabitating either.

"You have any other major bombs to drop today? Or this week?" Her words are light, playful even, as she asks.

The corners of my mouth tighten as the slightest smile starts to form. I shake my head. "No." I draw an *X* over my heart. "I swear."

"Best keep that promise, Kingsley." The moment she calls me Kingsley, every ounce of heaviness evaporates from my chest. "A girl can only handle so much at a time."

I lean in and press my lips to hers. "Sorry for my flabby lips. Can't seem to help myself with you."

"You're forgiven."

Twinkling green irises stare back at me as she continues to stroke my beard. I see her urge to answer, her need to relieve the anticipation in my veins. Knots twist beneath my diaphragm as I bite my tongue and wait for her to speak. I won't interrupt her moment. Won't pull the answer from her mind, her heart, her lips. I may speak more freely since Dad passed, but that doesn't mean everyone else does with the same level of ease.

"Yes," she whispers between us.

My eyes widen as a smile brightens her face. "Yes?" I ask, wanting to hear her answer again.

She nods. "Yes." Her voice bolder and more vibrant this time.

Without hesitation, I wrap her in my arms, roll onto my back and kiss her senseless. We laugh like giddy teenagers. Smile like lunatics. And goddamn, this is the best fucking feeling in the world. The woman I love is in my arms. The woman I love just agreed to move in together.

I am one lucky son of a bitch.

"Uh, Jameson."

I freeze at the slight seriousness in Penny's voice. "Yeah?"

"Can you take the condom off? It's all gross and weird." She chuckles. "And… we may need a new one soon."

I laugh and give her a quick squeeze before releasing her. "Anything for you, Queen of hearts." I kiss the tip of her nose. "Anything."

EPILOGUE
PENNY

November—two years later

THE DOORBELL RINGS AS I SLIDE THE SWEET POTATOES in the oven next to the cornbread casserole.

"I got it," Jameson says as he taps my ass and exits the kitchen.

"'Kay." I wipe my hands down my apron with a huff as I look around the kitchen. "Hot mess," I mumble to myself. "But we got this."

"Pen-Pen," a squealy voice calls from the living room. "Pen-Pen." Two little feet tap the tile as Ryker dashes around the counter and smacks into my legs, his little arms wrapping around me with all their might.

"Hey, little man." I bend and scoop up my nephew. "How's my favorite guy?"

"Hey!" Jameson teases as he enters the kitchen with Autumn, Jonas, and Clementine in tow.

I lean in close to Ryker and whisper in his ear. "Don't

94

tell uncle Jameson, but you'll always be my favorite." I wink at my husband and he shakes his head.

Ryker turns his head, cups his hands around my ear and whispers loud enough for the entire room to hear. "You're my favorite, Pen-Pen." The room fills with hushed laughter.

I set Ryker on his feet and kiss the top of his head. "I got out your coloring stuff, bud. Why don't you go make some awesome pictures for everyone."

He nods his little head with more energy than I've had all day. Clementine extends her hand to him and smiles. "C'mon, Ryker. Let's go color in the living room."

Bless Clementine and her patience with her little brother. Almost ten years stand between them, but she never acts as if he burdens her. She is the most attentive, loving big sister a sibling could ask for.

Although Jonas isn't her birth father, he treats her as if he were. And not long after Ryker was born, when Autumn and Jonas saw the edge of melancholy in Clementine, they all sat down and talked. Autumn told me that neither she nor Jonas bad-mouthed Clementine's birth father, but they didn't sugarcoat anything. That night, everything got laid out. Clementine and Autumn cried while Jonas held them both. In the end, Clementine discovered a new appreciation for her mother, the strength she held, and the loving family she now has, thanks to Jonas.

Most girls Clementine's age wouldn't enjoy coloring with their little brother. They would roll their eyes and go scroll through apps on their phones, ignoring everyone in the room for hours. But not Clementine. I rarely see her with a phone or device in her hand, and that is magical.

Autumn wraps me in her arms. "What can I help with?" With a step back, her eyes take in the kitchen and the apparent food explosion. "We brought apple and pumpkin pies."

Jonas lifts a reusable tote. "They don't need refrigeration."

"I'll show you where to set them," Jameson says. The guys amble into the attached dining room and Jameson shows Jonas the layout of the buffet setup.

"At this point, it's just cleanup."

My eyes glaze over as I take in the mess. Not a lick of counter space is clean. Flour and cornmeal. A partially used stick of butter, soft and unwrapped. Sweet potato skins and an empty marshmallow bag next to the bottle of maple syrup. Emptied cans and countless used utensils. Foil and plastic wrap and wax paper boxes. Hot mitts and trivets.

Thank goodness everyone is bringing something tonight. If I had to make any more than this, I'd never get out of the kitchen.

"We got this, Pen. Everything's in the oven?"

I nod. "Yep. Checked the turkey and ham before adding the sweet potatoes and cornbread."

Without another word, Autumn dives headfirst into cleanup mode and I follow suit. No matter how much time passes, no matter how different our lives are now, Autumn and I have always been a great team. Long-lost sisters.

Best friends. Always there for each other without question.

As I start on the dishes and Autumn wipes down the counter opposite me, the doorbell rings. Again and again. Over the next fifteen minutes, our closest friends and family trickle in for Friendsgiving. Each of them delivering a warm dish, hug and smile.

Jameson connects music to the wireless speakers, the volume loud enough to hear but quiet enough to not ruin conversations. Casserole dishes, cloth-covered baskets, and large pans fill the buffet as we all congregate near the dinner table.

When Jameson and I decided to move in together, we both agreed on a new place. Aside from rooming at Ricardo's, Jameson had been living with his mom on and off. Especially since his father passed. Although he didn't mind staying in the apartment from time to time, I knew it was time to move on.

After weeks of searching for the home that fit what we wanted—a house with enough space to accommodate guests and gatherings, but small enough to feel cozy and keep us humble—we hit the jackpot. A decent kitchen, a spacious dining and living room, and an expansive backyard—these were my only requests. Jameson's only request was three bedrooms and two bathrooms. Both our wishes came true two months into the search. Within three months, we were homeowners.

I scan the room, take note of all my favorite people in the same space.

Autumn, Jonas, Clementine and Ryker at the far end

of the table. Reznor, Tatyana, Ashton and Avery as they walk the buffet with whispered words. Rex and Giana, his girlfriend of one year—something none of us saw coming—huddled in the corner. Iliana and Sage—another unexpected, but good surprise—setting baskets of rolls in various spots on the tables. Cora, Gavin, Clara, and baby Garrett, the quietest baby I have ever laid eyes on. Micah and Peyton chatting with Shelly, Devlyn, and their sweet little Desirée. The rest of the King of Hearts crew—Chance, Frankie, Gage, Kennedy, and Ophelia. Jonas's friend, Trevor is arm in arm with Jillian, Jonas's baby sister. Jasmine, Anton, and little man Lex, still in his Superman costume from Halloween. And Peyton's former roommate, Reese, whispers in his husband, Trent's, ear as they fill plates with sweet potatoes and corn casserole.

At the head of the formal table, Jameson cuts the turkey while Enzo slices the ham, both lecturing the other on technique.

This right here—these people and their love—makes me whole. Seeing people I love gathered together, smiling and laughing and sharing, it gives me all the feels. The Sunday get-togethers we started almost six years ago have only grown. Some weeks, only ten of us gather. Other weeks, everyone shows up—parents included. Birthdays and holidays get extra attention, but as long as we spend time together, the occasion doesn't matter.

In a few days, we will all spend the holiday in different places. With family or just our significant others. But today is for all of us.

"Sweets." I snap my attention to my husband as he

ambles closer. He takes my hands in his and presses his lips to mine. "Everything okay?"

I nod. "Yeah. Everything's perfect." My hands trail up his chest and lock behind his neck. "Love you."

Another kiss. "Love you, too." He tips his head toward the table. "Let's join everyone."

We pile our plates high with a little bit of everything before taking our seats. Laughter and good conversation fill the room as we all catch up and talk about the upcoming holidays. When the food slowly disappears, we set the kids up with a movie in the living room while the adults sit outside by the fire. It all feels so familiar, yet completely new.

Years ago, I never would have seen myself here. In this house or this life. But when this man, the handsome one with his arm around my shoulders, stepped back into my life, I knew it would be nothing like I pictured it. He isn't just my brother's best friend. He isn't just the guy I had an epic crush on as a girl. No, this man is so much more.

My soul mate. The missing piece that kept me from getting serious with anyone.

My King.

And the day he asked me to be his forever, the word yes couldn't spill from my lips fast enough. My eyes fall to my hand on his thigh. To the vintage-style ring on my left fourth finger. To the pink pear-shaped diamond that has to be at least a carat. And the countless white diamonds set in the rose gold band.

Before Jameson, I never saw myself married. I never imagined the flashy ring on my finger or the handsome man on my arm who can't kiss me enough. Our marriage may be young—only nine months now—but it feels as if I have finally come home. It finally feels like I belong.

Jameson Kingsley is more than my husband. He is the sun and the stars. The dusk and the dawn. My beginning and end. The King of my heart.

I snuggle into his side more and kiss the spot beneath his ear. "I love you, King."

He twists until our eyes lock, pins me in place for three breaths, cups my cheek, and kisses me as if no one else exists. "I love you, Queen. Forever."

The Click Duet

High school sweethearts torn apart. When fate gives them a second chance, one doesn't trust they won't be hurt again. Through the Lens (Click Duet #1) and Time Exposure (Click Duet #2) is an angsty, second chance, friends to lovers romance with all the feels.

The Inked Duet

A man with a broken heart and a woman scared to put herself out there. Love is never easy. Sometimes love rips you apart. Fine Line (Inked Duet #1) and Love Buzz (Inked Duet #2) is a second chance at love, single parent romance with a pinch of angst and dash of suspense.

The Insomniac Duet

He was her high school bully. She was the outcast that secretly crushed on him. More than ten years later, he's her boss, completely oblivious to their shared past, and wants no one but her. More importantly, he doesn't understand her animosity toward him.

The Artist Duet

A tortured hero with the biggest heart and a charismatic heroine with the patience of a saint. Previous heartache has him fighting his desire to be more than friends with her. But she is everywhere, and he can't help but give in. The Artist Duet is an angsty, friends to lovers slow burn.

Transcendental

A musician in search of his muse and a woman grieving the loss of her husband. Two weeks at an exclusive retreat and their connection rivals all others. Until she leaves early without notice. But he refuses to give up until he finds her again.

Distorted Devotion

Swept off her feet by love, life takes a dark, unexpected turn. Now the love of her life may be the cause of her death. Check out this gripping, romantic suspense.

Depths Awakened

A small town romance which captivates you from the start. Two broken souls have sworn off love. Vowed to never lose anyone else. But their undeniable attraction brings them together and refuses to let go.

Broken Metronome

When the music of the heart dies…

Broken Metronome is an angsty poetry collection full of heartache and the possibility of what may have been.

Slipping From Existence

Would it be so bad to slip from existence? Would it be so bad to give in to the darkness?

Slipping From Existence is a dark poetry collection centered around depression and coping while maintaining a brave face.

THANK YOU

Thank you so much for reading **Penny,** a Bay Area Duet Series novella. If you wouldn't mind taking a moment to leave a review on the retailer site where you made your purchase, Goodreads and/or BookBub, it would mean the world to me.

Reviews help other readers find and enjoy the book as well.

Much love,
Persephone

ACKNOWLEDGMENTS

To my family and friends… Your continued support of my books is my greatest joy. Thank you for always cheering me on! I love you the mostest!

To Ellie McLove and Rosa Sharon… Thanks for always performing magic when I hand you my word babies. Just when I think I have punctuation down… wrong! You're rockstars and I am grateful for you both! And thanks for always putting love notes in the margins. xoxo

To my author friends… All the hugs! This author thing isn't all rainbows and sunshine, but having you in my circle and corner makes each day better. Love you all!

To the readers and bloggers who read my words… sending you all virtual hugs. Every time I read one of your amazing reviews or see your posts about my books, I cry. Spilling pieces of yourself on paper isn't easy, but your kindness makes it so worth it each time I start a new book. A million thank yous to each of you!

And if this is your first Persephone Autumn story… thank you for taking a chance on my words. I hope you loved Penny and Jameson.

ABOUT THE AUTHOR

Persephone Autumn lives in Florida with her wife, crazy dog, and two lover-boy cats. A proud mom with a cuckoo grandpup. An ethnic food enthusiast who has fun discovering ways to vegan-ize her favorite non-vegan foods. If given the opportunity, she would intentionally get lost in nature.

For years, Persephone did some form of writing; mostly journaling or poetry. After pairing her poetry with images and posting them online, she began the journey of writing her first novel.

She mainly writes romance and poetry, but on occasion dips her toes in other works. Look for her non-romance publications under P. Autumn.